A VINEYARD QUILT MYSTERY™

THREADS OF DECEIT

MAE ··· DS

Annie's®
AnniesCraftStore.com

Library of Congress-in-Publication Data
Threads of Deceit / by Mae Fox & Jan Fields
p. cm.
I. Title

2014915926

AnniesCraftStore.com
(800) 282-6643
A Vineyard Quilt Mystery™
Series Creator: Shari Lohner
Series Editors: Shari Lohner, Janice Tate, and Ken Tate
Cover Illustrator: Kelley McMorris

10 11 12 13 14 | Printed in China | 9 8 7 6 5 4 3 2 1

PROLOGUE

Rain spattered against the empty street that stank of wet pavement and something less pleasant ... sewage, mold, and a pinch of death. A tall woman pulled the hood of her long coat farther forward to hide her face. The picture of hunched misery, she kept to the shadows and walked close to the buildings as if hoping for a shield from the damp onslaught.

Nearly a block ahead, a rotund man stomped his way down the sidewalk, splashing as he went. His black umbrella and neatly pressed pants, now a muddy ruin at the cuffs, gave him a subtle English air. He clutched a small wrapped package to his chest. Never pausing or glancing backward, he gave no sign that he was aware of the woman's pursuit.

Though she felt edgy, creeping along as she did, the woman didn't allow that to quicken her steps or close the distance between them. This wasn't her first time following a stranger on a rainy night.

The man stopped so suddenly that she nearly stumbled in surprise. She ducked into the small alcove of a shop entrance, where the darkness that pooled around the door covered her completely. The man turned then, his movements stiff. His gaze swept over the street and sidewalk but didn't linger on her hiding place.

His umbrella shook, revealing his nerves. He turned away and darted around the corner. The woman sprang out of the shadows and ran after him, grateful for the soft-soled shoes that kept her footfalls from ringing against the wet pavement. She reached the corner and peeked around the stained brickwork of the old building. She saw the man pressed against a door, his shoulders hunched against the rain as he fumbled with a lock. In a flash, he ducked into the building.

"Bingo," the woman whispered.

"Bingo what?" the voice in her ear came so suddenly and so loud that the woman jumped.

"I found his stash," she whispered, trying to regain her composure.

"Excellent! Do you want to call the police or shall I?"

"I'll do it." She paused. "After I retrieve the client's property."

A groan grated against her eardrum. "Julie Ellis, are you out of your mind? We had an agreement. You find the stash, and then we let the police recover the stolen loot."

"I didn't argue with you," Julie said quietly. "But that's not the same as agreeing."

"Why do you always do this? You're going to get yourself killed one of these days!"

"Look, Hannah, I can't call yet. If I do, that Imari *Kakiemon* porcelain vase will end up sitting in an evidence locker somewhere for who knows how long. How much time do you think the old woman has left to live?"

"I know your heart is in the right place—"

"No. No argument. The whole reason the vase has been missing for seventy years is because the *authorities* lost the family heirloom when they rounded up one little girl's entire family and shipped them off to an internment camp. How can I face the family and say that I left their vase in the hands of the *authorities* again?"

"You can't run around breaking and entering and tampering with a crime scene."

"It's not a crime scene until the police show up."

"It doesn't work like that, and you know it." Hannah's voice was filled with urgency. "Now call the police and get back here."

"I'm having trouble hearing you, Hannah," Julie said, tugging the Bluetooth headset out of her ear. She held it in front of her mouth for a moment. "It must be this rain ... bad reception ... sorry." She dropped the receiver into her pocket.

The door she was watching opened, and the man stepped out. Julie ducked around the corner and into a doorway again. She pressed herself tightly against the cold metal of the door, breathing shallowly in the thick air.

Moments later, the man strode around the corner. There was no sign of the package. He held his umbrella at a slight angle, blocking his side vision. Still, Julie held her breath, willing him to pass without glancing her way. He did.

When his footsteps faded, she stepped out of the shadows and smiled. Time for her favorite part of the evening—a little breaking and entering for a good cause.

ONE

S*ix months later.*

The black Buick Verano slipped smoothly out of the bustle of late-season tourist traffic and slowed to a stop at the curb. The two women in the car leaned forward to peer out the front window at the tall, red brick Victorian perched on the low hill. Everything about the house was neat: the clean lines between cream and blue painted trim, the precision of the old brickwork, the way the tall peaked turret seemed to jab at the clouds floating by in the late summer sky.

Forty-year-old Julie Ellis smiled at the house, thinking it was a perfect match for the woman beside her. Hannah Marks had that same precision about her, that same orderliness. She liked order and rules and systems. She would fit in perfectly at the Quilt Haus Inn. Julie, on the other hand, knew she might find that her own square peg had a bit more trouble cramming into any available round hole.

Hannah leaned back into her seat and pushed her glasses up on her nose. "This is never going to work."

"What?" Julie pulled her eyes away from the house and flipped down the driver's-side visor. She ran a hand through her dark curls, hoping they were properly tamed. She needed to look the very soul of virtue. *Maybe a bun?* She looked around for a pencil to hold the bun in place.

"You playing innkeeper. You'll be organizing high-stakes poker matches with the elderly quilters by the end of the week just to stir things up."

"First, not all quilters are elderly," Julie said, squinting as she peered at her lips. Should she put on a bright "atta girl" lipstick or go for the innocent, natural look?

"That's not relevant."

Julie continued as if Hannah hadn't spoken. "And second, I happen to *like* quilting. I haven't had much time for it, but I'm looking forward to having that chance now."

"Right … I give it four days before the first casino night. That's assuming you even get the job."

"I'll get it. I always get what I go after."

Hannah rolled her eyes at that, looking suddenly younger than her normally stern thirty-something. "I applaud your choice of a non-larcenous career change, but this job is going to bore you to tears."

"No job is boring if you do it right. And I plan to do this one right."

"So you're committed to this."

"I am."

"And you honestly believe it's going to work."

"I do."

"Come on, Julie. We're in Straussberg, Missouri. *Missouri!*" Hannah pulled a handful of paper from her oversized tote. "Allow me to read from the riveting visitor's information guide: 'A picturesque nineteenth-century village filled with friendly people, strong family values, and beautiful, river valley surroundings. A destination spot for tourists drawn to its antique shops, quaint wineries, German heritage, and grand historic homes.'"

"I like antiques."

"You steal antiques."

Julie turned sharply toward her friend. "I liberate them from thieves and return them to their true owners. Or I *did* anyway. I didn't steal, not morally. And I don't do any of that anymore. I'm an innkeeper now. Besides, I don't need you to tell me about Straussberg. I've been here before."

Hannah looked at Julie in surprise. "You have not."

"I have."

"I've worked with you for ten years. Our recovery jobs have taken us to New York City, London, even Rome—but never Missouri. I would have remembered."

"It was before I got into the antiquities recovery business. Long before you became my assistant."

Silence pooled in the car for a moment.

Finally, Hannah said, "We're not here for any reason you haven't told me, are we?"

"We're here because our last job upset some very nasty people, as you well know."

"Which it wouldn't have if you'd just called the police."

Julie groaned. "Yes, yes, you were right. But we need to remember the important thing—that I recovered the vase and made one dying grandmother very happy."

"Somehow I think the fact that you were almost killed qualifies for the 'important thing' status," Hannah said.

Julie waved that away. "I'm fine. And now the important thing is that Straussberg is the perfect place to start a new, less-dangerous career, which is something you've often said you wanted."

"I'm not sure hiding from international art thieves is really that much less dangerous, but I'll agree that this looks like the last place they'd come looking for you. Of course, that assumes you'll let Straussberg remain a nice quiet village. You do like to stir things up."

"Only when they need stirring."

"I feel the inevitable end of us being chased out of town with pitchforks and torches drawing near."

Julie gave her friend a smile that made Hannah moan in

despair. Then she hopped out and headed up the wide steps cut into the hillside.

It was time to start her new life.

As she approached the house, she couldn't help but admire the lavish gingerbread trim and the way the paint drew the eye to every detail. The plantings around the tall Victorian were minimal to allow the building to shine. Julie slowed her pace as she climbed the steps to the small front porch, where rocking chairs waited for guests to sit and enjoy the warm day. Upon closer inspection, she saw signs of wear in the mortar between the bricks and the faded paint on the porch supports. But it was still a beautiful old house.

Julie strode into the front foyer, sizing up the small woman standing by the front desk. The iron-gray curls and dainty glasses perched on her nose gave the woman a storybook grandmotherly look. But Julie also recognized the hint of steely determination in the way the woman stood and in the tilt of her chin. A person would be ill advised to underestimate her.

"Welcome to the Quilt Haus Inn," the older woman said.

"Thank you. I'm Julie Ellis. Are you Millie Rogers?"

The woman's sharp gaze swept over Julie in an instant, her polite smile never wavering. "I am." Then she looked past Julie to Hannah, offering a befuddled look that Julie didn't believe for an instant. She had a hunch Millie knew exactly how to play the slightly confused old lady. "Goodness, I didn't realize I had *two* applicants coming today."

"Only one applicant, I'm afraid," Julie said. "This is Hannah Marks, my research assistant. You see, I'm writing a book on the history of quilting in America. I saw the ad for an onsite manager for your lovely inn, and I thought the job would be perfect for me. I love organizing things and meeting new people. And I'm wild about antiques and quilting."

Millie raised one thin eyebrow. "This job will require a great deal of your time. We have a fairly small staff—basically a cook, a housekeeper, and Shirley, who runs the tearoom and fabric shop. They've all been here nearly as long as I have. Shirley and the housekeeper will be a huge help to whomever I hire, but the new innkeeper will need to be prepared to pitch in whenever and wherever is needed."

"I don't mind work," Julie said.

"In addition, you'd be expected to register the guests and plan all of the special events. As you are aware, we cater mainly to quilters. They expect a high level of service. If you're trying to divide your time between a book project and the work of the inn, I'm not certain that would be appropriate."

Julie's smile never wavered. "I barely devote an hour or two a week to writing. Poor Hannah despairs of my ever getting the book done, I'm sure. But I have plenty of hours in the day for the job here. I wouldn't consider applying otherwise."

Millie frowned slightly. "It has been hard enough for me to accept the fact that I'm running out of time on this earth and retire. I don't plan to sit around counting the hairs on my cat's head or talking to my plants. I'm going to travel, and I won't always be easy to reach if things go wrong here. I need someone I can trust completely."

"I hope to convince you that I *am* that person," Julie said. "I would so enjoy being back here in Straussberg. My mother was raised here. Perhaps you knew her since you share a last name. Adelaide Rogers?"

Millie's eyes opened wide with what was clearly genuine surprise. "I had no idea that Addie had a child."

"That's understandable. My mother didn't believe in hanging on to the past. She said her marriage to my father cut a lot of old ties."

Millie sighed. "Your mother was a beautiful child and sweet in her own way, but she was a wild one. Her marriage to Bertram Ellis was simply the straw that broke a very shaky camel's back. I'm not saying I condone the way the family treated her, but I suppose I do understand it."

Julie's smile tightened. "That makes one of us. At any rate, I know family history can be complicated, but my parents are gone now, and that's another reason for my interest in the area. I want to experience the land where my mother grew up. And I would do a good job for you here. I assume we're related somehow?"

"Our kinship is rather distant. But I suppose you *are* family. ..." Millie's face reflected a flutter of emotions until it finally locked on one. "You can have the job. When can you start?"

"I'm ready right this moment," Julie said. "But any time after that is fine too."

Millie turned to look at Hannah again. "Do you need additional rooms for your friend?"

Hannah smiled. "I will probably rent a room closer into town. I have the names of a few places. First, I'm going to find a job of my own. My work researching leaves me with a lot of spare time as well." She paused. "Do you know anyone hiring a sous chef? I can also do short-order cooking. I'm not proud."

Millie's sharp eyes lit with interest. "You can cook?"

"I worked for two years in a small Amish restaurant in Pennsylvania," Hannah said. "And before that, I worked a number of months as a short-order cook in a little diner. My specialty, though, is pastry, but I assumed it would be easier to get a sous chef job at first."

"As it happens, our cook is leaving," Millie said. "Like

me, she's retiring, though for different reasons. The poor old dear has health issues. Personally, I'm trying to get out of this place before I *get* health issues." She laughed dryly at that. "At any rate, if you're interested, we could try you out. You would fix breakfast most days and a larger brunch on Sunday. You'd also do some baking for the tearoom, but I imagine you would still have some time to research your book."

Hannah glanced at Julie and was rewarded by a bright smile. "That sounds wonderful, doesn't it, Hannah?"

"It does. I would love to give it a try."

Millie rubbed her hands together. "Marvelous. We have some house specialties you'll need to learn, but I can show you those, and you'll have Inga Mehl's help, of course. She's our housekeeper, but she lends a hand in the kitchen in the mornings. She's not chatty, but she's extremely competent, and loyal to a fault." Millie's smile flashed between Julie and Hannah. "I can't believe my good luck, filling two positions at once! Let me show you both to your rooms."

"Sounds good," Julie said.

Millie took them on a tour of the old mansion, clearly very proud of her inn. Her initial reticence seemed to be completely gone, and she chattered about the history of the Quilt Haus Inn, stopping frequently to point out specific items and tell stories associated with each. When a guest finally interrupted them to ask Millie a question, it was a relief to slip away to collect their luggage.

Hannah swung a heavy suitcase from the trunk of Julie's car, then slung a duffle over her shoulder. "So, how much of that family story was true?"

"I never lie," Julie said, "about family."

"Have you considered what you're going to do when she wonders why you don't actually write a book? Which brings me to another question: Why claim to be a writer?"

Julie shrugged. "Sometimes I like to ask nosy questions. People expect that of writers. And if we ever have to … leave suddenly, we'll have an excuse to fall back on. We can tell Millie that we got a big offer on the book and now have to go write full time."

"And you're thinking we might have to leave suddenly?"

"You never know. I like to be prepared. Besides, who knows? Maybe I *will* write a book." Julie hauled her own sleek black luggage from the car and turned to head for her new home. "I'll have to do *something* to keep things interesting."

"That's exactly what has me worried," Hannah grumbled.

Two

Within six weeks, Julie and Hannah had mastered their new roles so well that Millie applauded herself on their hire every time she dropped by the inn. Not that she did so often. She made an appearance now and again between the post-cards she sent from virtually every attraction in Missouri, some of which Julie had no idea existed. Julie had gotten cards from the Jesse James Home, Talking Rocks Cavern, and Leila's Hair Museum. Hannah declared the last one just plain creepy.

Julie found that the innkeeper's job tested her skills in diplomacy and her personal depths in patience. She often thought back to how she'd told Hannah she was certain the job wouldn't be dull, but some days, a little dullness would have been a nice change.

"At my age, I simply cannot suffer that kind of heat!" Mrs. Cantrell's shrill voice jerked Julie out of her reverie. The old woman thrust her head forward, peering with dark eyes through her slightly smudged glasses. "Last night, I nearly *died* of heatstroke."

Mrs. Cantrell's twin sister, Miss Lawson, shuddered, setting the feather on her floppy round hat quivering. "We never imagined the third floor could be so beastly hot."

Julie's suite was also on the third floor, and she didn't find it disagreeable, but she knew arguing with the guests never turned out well. "I'll be happy to turn up the air conditioning on the third floor."

The sisters turned their matching horrified expressions toward Julie, and for a moment, she was reminded of two owls with ruffled feathers. She half expected them to hoot.

"Oh no," Miss Lawson said. "It's not healthful to breathe artificial air."

"Our neighbor put in one of those horrible air conditioners," Mrs. Cantrell said. "She was dead within the month."

"Her son insisted it was smoking that got her, but she lived through years of smoking and then died within the month of getting the air conditioner." Miss Lawson leaned in conspiratorially. "It's no mystery what *really* caused her death. We try not to go anywhere with an air conditioner."

"Which isn't easy," Mrs. Cantrell added, and the sisters bobbed their heads in unison.

"I'm sure it isn't," Julie said. "Maybe you could open the windows in your bedroom? Since you have the tower bedroom, you should get a nice cross ventilation."

Mrs. Cantrell shook her head. "We don't care for open windows. All sorts of pollen can blow in. My sinuses are quite delicate."

"They are indeed," Miss Lawson affirmed. "And I have ghastly allergies."

"I could bring up a fan?" Julie suggested.

"And blow the heat around!" Miss Lawson flapped her hands in distress. "We might as well sleep in a convection oven."

"You do have the oddest ideas," Mrs. Cantrell added, though she gave Julie a gentle pat on the arm to soften the remark.

For a fleeting moment, Julie had a warm, wistful longing for the days when the greatest conflicts in her life came from gun-wielding bad guys. At least she could hit them. She sighed softly. "Do you have any ideas to suggest?"

The sisters responded with a sharp-eyed glare. "It's not

our job to figure out how to do *yours*," Mrs. Cantrell said. "But the heat on the third floor is simply unacceptable."

Julie stretched a painful smile. "I could move you to the second floor. We have one remaining empty suite on the second floor."

Miss Lawson narrowed her eyes and thrust her pointed nose closer to Julie. "We wouldn't want to pay a higher rate."

"We can't just throw money around," Mrs. Cantrell added.

"No, no, I'll let you have it for the same rate," Julie said.

The sisters looked at each other, then back at Julie. They gave a decisive nod in unison.

"Fine," Miss Lawson said. "We're going to get breakfast now. Tell us when our new room is ready."

"Of course," Julie said.

As the matching set of old ladies strutted away, their heads tilting toward each other, Julie heard one last sharp comment: "The inn was much better when Millie was here."

Great, Julie thought as she wondered exactly how Millie would have magically controlled the unseasonably hot Missouri fall weather.

With her smile still pasted on, Julie walked through the open French doors and into the airy breakfast room. It was the largest public area in the inn, matching the size of the huge remodeled kitchen at the back of the house.

She wove through the tables with their crisp white cloths, pausing at each to make a friendly comment or ask a question. To her joy, no one else had a complaint to share with her. When she finally reached the back of the room, she turned and looked over the full tables, and her smile grew easier. The inn was nearly full. In fact, with the sisters moving to the second floor, now the only open suite was on the third floor. Normally, Millie didn't rent out the third-floor suite. She saved it for family or friends visiting. Or when they needed a room in an emergency. The only reason the twin sisters had been in the suite was because they'd especially asked for it to enjoy the quiet.

Julie's smile turned wry. *Figures.* The important thing was that the inn was doing well.

She turned her gaze from the people filling the impeccably clean breakfast room to the furniture and floors. She could see wear on the seats of the dining room chairs. She should discuss re-covering them with Millie.

She'd seen a lot of little things like that—floors that could use refinishing, drapes with missing fringe, bathroom fixtures that seemed to require a bit too much fiddling to work. None of the things made the guests' experience unpleasant, but Julie worried about the accumulated worn look. Nothing draws business like success, and worn dining room chairs didn't scream success.

Julie made a mental note to create a list, prioritizing the things that needed attention first. She could talk about it with Millie, and they could work out a slow but steady plan for upgrading. She might even tackle a few items herself.

Julie reached the long breakfast buffet table. Cinnamon and spice from the basket of muffins made her stomach growl, even though she'd snuck one of those very muffins from the kitchen earlier.

The sharp sizzle of melting butter drew Julie's attention to the pan Hannah swirled. With great fanfare, she broke an egg into the hot butter and mixed them together.

Julie edged closer. "That looks delicious."

"It is," Hannah said with a smile. The eggs began to turn color immediately. Gently loosening the edge of the omelet, she added cheese and sautéed mushrooms, then expertly flipped the omelet closed and slid it onto a plate before handing it to a bespectacled man who stood beside his plump, cheerful wife. The woman held a plate piled high with fruit. The couple cooed over the omelet and hurried off to their table.

"Have you seen Inga recently?" Julie asked, scanning the room for any sign of the housekeeper. "I need her to move the sisters out of the tower suite and down to the second floor."

Hannah nodded. "As far as I know, she's cleaning up in the kitchen. But that woman is practically a ghost. Half the time I don't hear her come or go. All I see is the perfect cleanliness and order left in her wake."

"I suppose that's the best kind of ghost to have." Stepping behind the breakfast table, Julie slipped through a door marked with a "Staff Only" sign. She walked down the hallway, past the door to the inn's cellar and on to the kitchen. As always, stepping through the swinging door was like entering a different world. As much as Millie loved the antiques in the rest of the inn, she'd gone all out to make the kitchen modern and efficient.

The only antique-looking thing in the room was Inga Mehl, who carefully loaded the dishwasher. Not that Inga was more than fifty, but her dark hair was streaked with gray, and she always wore shades of gray, drab colors that seemed to match her expressionless solemnity. It gave her the look of a woman from a different time.

"Inga?" Julie said, annoyed to hear the hesitancy in her own voice. "The guests in the tower want to move down to the empty suite on the second floor. Can you handle that this morning?"

Inga nodded. "I can do that now, Miss Ellis."

Julie repressed a sigh. She'd already asked the housekeeper

to call her Julie several times. "Thank you."

Julie backed up, ducking into the hallway. She felt an instant relief as soon as Inga's dark, disapproving eyes were no longer pointed her way. The woman was an amazing worker, but she reminded Julie of the ominous housekeepers who populated gothic literature.

Julie hurried back to the breakfast room, pausing at the buffet table to paste a warm smile on her face.

"You don't fool me, you know," Hannah said.

"And how am I trying to fool you this time?" Julie asked.

"All that smiling. I can see the cabin fever setting in, making you all squinchy around the eyes."

"I'm fairly certain 'squinchy' is not a real word," Julie said mildly. "But I'm delighted to see this new whimsical, imaginative side of you, Hannah. Perhaps *you're* the one who should take up writing a book."

"So you're perfectly happy as an innkeeper?"

"Perfectly." Julie resisted the urge to add that she was simply creeped out by her housekeeper as she waited for Hannah's next remark, but it never came.

Instead, Hannah looked over Julie's right shoulder, and her eyes widened. Julie turned to follow Hannah's gaze and saw that a newcomer had entered the dining room. Men tended to be in the minority at the Quilt Haus Inn, and this particular man couldn't have looked less like a quilter if he'd tried. His darkly tanned skin made it clear he spent a lot of time outside, and his broad shoulders filled out his shirt in a way that suggested the time spent was active. Julie narrowed her eyes, wondering if he might be someone sent to track her down. If so, she needed to get him away from the inn's guests as quickly as possible.

Julie pulled what she hoped was a welcoming smile onto

her face and quickly crossed the room. "Welcome to the Quilt Haus Inn. How can I help you this morning?"

He returned her smile, his eyes crinkling with laugh lines baked into the skin. "I'm looking for a room."

"I'm sorry. We cater primarily to quilters."

He raised a single dark eyebrow. "How do you know I'm not a quilter?"

"You look like someone who spends his time doing something more ... athletic than stitching quilts."

His smile stretched still farther. "Looks can be deceiving." He turned and pointed to each of the framed quilt blocks that hung on the walls of the breakfast room and began to name the block designs. "Old Maid's Puzzle, Pinwheel, Rail Fence, Spool, Shoo Fly, Pieced Star, Dutchman's Puzzle, and Churn Dash." Then he stepped back out into the foyer and pointed at the full-size quilts that hung from the walls. "Drunkard's Path, Victorian Crazy Quilting, done in the traditional velvets—very nice, Double Wedding Ring. And this last one isn't actually quilting at all." He gestured to a coverlet done in jewel tones and black. "Cathedral Squares."

He turned back to Julie, a twinkle in his gray-blue eyes. "So can I rent a room?"

Julie blinked, finding his intense gaze more than a little unnerving. "I stand corrected. You clearly know a great deal about quilts." Even so, she wasn't particularly comforted. Someone in the business of stealing antiquities might have all kinds of unusual knowledge.

"I'm full of surprises."

Julie made a noncommittal sound and strode to the front desk. The man followed close behind.

She opened the ledger. "I'm afraid the only suite available is on the third floor. It's the tower room. Both the room and the bath are smaller than what's offered in the second-floor suites, and there is no separate sitting area." Julie offered a discouraging frown.

"I don't need a lot of room." He pulled a credit card from his wallet and held it out to her.

Julie looked down at the credit card, then up at him. "I'm also told it's swelteringly hot up there. You might be more comfortable at the inn down the street, Mr. ...?"

"Franklin. But call me Daniel, please. And I'm not worried about the heat." Daniel wiggled his credit card in the air. "I'll open a window. I've been in hotter places, I'm sure."

Julie smiled tightly and took the card. She gestured behind her toward the breakfast room. "The only meal we offer is breakfast. On Sundays, we have a more extensive buffet, and the hours we serve are extended." Then she turned to nod toward the other set of French doors on the opposite side of the foyer from the breakfast room. "We have a small quilt shop, which also serves tea and pastries throughout the day. Anything you need for your quilting project, you should be able to find there. If we don't have it, our shop manager, Shirley, can definitely find it for you. She's positively magic that way." Julie finalized the transaction and pushed the guest ledger toward him to sign, still wary of his story. Over the years, she'd developed a fairly accurate sense about people. And something about Daniel Franklin didn't add up.

"So I'm *officially* booked into my room?" he asked.

"Yes, though the room isn't ready yet. I can store your luggage if you like and have it taken up to the room by two o'clock at the latest. Until then, you're welcome to use any of the public rooms down here."

"As long as I'm official, and you can't back out, I suppose I should come clean."

Julie tensed, wishing she had some kind of makeshift weapon at her disposal besides a ballpoint pen adorned with a spool of thread. Surely he wasn't simply going to admit he'd come to exact revenge for her interfering in the art theft ring's business, was he? "Come clean about what, Mr. Franklin?"

"I'm not actually a quilter."

Julie gulped. "What are you?"

"I'm a historian. My focus is on American arts, which is how I know all those quilt patterns. I've looked at a lot of historically significant quilts during my career."

"I see." Julie didn't know whether to laugh or cry. "So, are you on the trail of a rare quilt?"

"No. I'm tracking something much bigger."

Again Julie felt a frisson of worry. Was he toying with her? She didn't say anything, but merely raised an eyebrow.

His grin grew. "I've come to find the final resting place of *The Grand Adventure*, a side-wheeler steamboat that sank over a hundred and fifty years ago on its first trip up the Missouri River."

Julie's unease was immediately replaced by curiosity. "I don't see any diving equipment," she said. "I think you'll have trouble renting it locally. We don't have a lot of people diving in the river around here."

He shook his head. "No diving required. I'm going to be hunting for this steamboat in the middle of a farm field. And if I'm right, I'm going to find a treasure in the process!"

THREE

Late in the afternoon, Julie ducked into the brightly lit kitchen to grab a moment's peace and a cup of coffee. As much as she enjoyed the antiques throughout the inn, she found the kitchen's gleaming stainless steel counters and high-end appliances soothing. They reminded her of her New York City loft.

All of the countertops matched the stainless steel finish on the fridge and stove—except for a single slab of marble in the baking area. Julie thought it looked odd, but Hannah told her marble was naturally colder, so it made a great surface for rolling out pastry dough.

As Julie crossed the room, Hannah looked up from a recipe book she was reading. "I'm looking for a different recipe for *pfeffernüsse*; the one I have doesn't taste right."

"I don't actually know what that is." Julie opened a cupboard and pulled out her favorite mug. It didn't match the lovely cream-colored mugs the guests used. This mug had been a gift from the mentor who had taught her all about antiquities recovery—and helped her to become a very successful antiques bounty hunter. The mug was tall and thick with "Never Get Caught" printed in white on the chocolate-brown glaze.

"They look a little like Danish wedding cookies, but they're spicier. I can't seem to get them right."

Julie wrinkled her nose as she turned to the basket that held all the different coffee pods for the shiny single-cup coffee maker. "I don't like anything covered in powdered sugar—too messy."

"There is that," Hannah said. "I doubt Inga would enjoy cleaning powdered sugar off the floor of the tearoom. Maybe I should omit the *pfeffernüsse* and add *Lebkuchen* instead."

Julie put a hand to her hip. "Now you're just showing off. I assume that's a cookie?"

Hannah nodded. "Despite your crabby responses to my cookie problem, you look cheerier overall. Did the sisters fall into the Missouri?"

"No," Julie said as she popped her chosen pod into the coffee maker. The shiny black-and-chrome appliance was the one item they'd saved when they closed the New York office. Hannah had insisted they bring it, and Julie had to admit she would have missed it too. "I'm disappointed that you think seeing those sweet little old ladies fall into the river would make me happy. They're perfectly nice." For a moment, she was glad her nose couldn't actually grow from the whopper she'd just told.

Hannah shoved an envelope into the cookbook for a bookmark and walked over to the counter. "Something has put a spring in your step. Let me see if I can guess. ..."

Julie sipped from her steaming cup. "I could just be happy for no particular reason, you know."

"Right." Hannah thought for a moment, then smiled mischievously. "I know what's caused the roses in your cheeks—our newest quilter."

"He's not a quilter. He tricked me a little there."

"Wow, a trickster. He sounds perfect for you."

"Snarkiness is not one of your more appealing traits."

Hannah waved off the criticism. "So tell me some more about our sneaky new guest who has you so chipper."

Julie leaned on the counter, her long fingers wrapped around the warm mug. "He is a historian on a treasure hunt.

Apparently he figured out the location of an old steamship wreck, *The Grand Adventure*."

"Let me guess—you're planning to dive on the wreck and beat him to the treasure?"

"No. First, I wouldn't do that. And second, it's not under water. At least, Daniel doesn't think it is. He believes it's buried on a farm here."

"'Daniel'? How quickly we've reached a first-name basis."

Julie shook her head. "Hannah Marks, what has gotten into you? You know I'm not interested in romance."

"Sure," Hannah said. "Because you're not human or anything like that."

Julie took a sip of her coffee while she glared at her friend over the top of her cup. Finally, she let her well of enthusiasm bubble over. "This *is* exciting stuff. As I was helping him with his luggage, Daniel told me that he's going to be excavating on the Winkler farm, and he expects to find some impressive pre–Civil War artifacts. Somehow or other, I plan to be involved with this."

"Sure, because getting involved in a treasure hunt is a great way to lay low and avoid the attention of certain people who would love to find you."

"I'll be careful."

Hannah rolled her eyes. "Right, like you always are. And I just finished unpacking the last of my stuff."

"Good, because we're not going anywhere. I *will* be careful." Julie drew an imaginary cross over her heart with one finger. She took another sip of her coffee just as Shirley Ott popped her head through the kitchen door. As always, the plump tea shop manager's plume of bright red hair added several inches to her height.

"Oh, Julie, there you are. Could you come and give me

a hand in the tearoom? One of our guests only drinks white tea infused at seventy degrees. I have no idea how to do that."

Julie looked at Hannah. "Thermometer?"

"I have a high-tech infrared one. That should impress them." Hannah rooted in a drawer and handed Julie something that looked like a small gun. "Just point at the water and shoot."

"If you say so." Julie followed Shirley's colorful form back to the tearoom. The tearoom manager could be counted upon to choose outfits every bit as vibrant as her red hair. Today she'd matched a handmade patchwork skirt in bright jewel tones with a fringed scarf shot through with gold threads.

Shirley's attire never ceased to amaze Julie. The older woman clearly loved color, and her outfits also reflected her amazing sewing and quilting skills. Shirley proudly admitted she'd designed and made nearly every item in her wardrobe.

Together, they soon had the picky guest calmed down and happily sipping her perfectly brewed tea. Julie stood near the counter in the retail area with Shirley and looked around the room. The racks of fabrics and notions were impeccably neat as always. Most of the small group of tables had someone sitting, sipping tea, and nibbling on one of Hannah's amazing baked goods.

"It's busy today," Julie said.

"Thanks to the gossip." Shirley spoke in what she probably thought was a whisper, but since she was slightly hard of hearing, her whispers tended to carry.

Julie looked at her in surprise. "What gossip?"

"About the discovery of a steamboat on the Winklers' farm," Shirley said, her blue eyes sparkling. "With treasure, no less! It's the talk of the town. And what a marvelous name—*The Grand Adventure*. Who can resist an adventure?"

Julie looked at her in speechless amazement, and Shirley laughed. "My dear, there is one absolute truth about this lovely town. I've lived here my whole life, and I can tell you that we are chockablock with good old-fashioned busybodies, of which I am the commander-in-chief. We were connected long before there was an Internet, and texting just makes us even faster. Nothing beats the speed of the Straussberg gossip network."

Julie couldn't help but be amused by the cheerful woman's complete comfort with her role as house gossip.

Shirley leaned closer to Julie and said, "I'm glad you're here. I wanted to tell you something."

"Oh?"

"I heard about the twins giving you a hard time. You mustn't let them bother you."

Julie stiffened slightly and considered hushing the smiling woman. She certainly didn't want the guests in the tearoom to hear her gossiping with Shirley. Then the older woman patted her arm solicitously. "They have gotten their room moved every year they've come here. They always insist on the third-floor room because of the quiet. Then they complain about the heat and end up being moved to the second floor while still paying the cheaper rate. It's a tradition, actually."

"Really?" Julie was so stunned that she forgot about her worry over Shirley's loud whispers.

Shirley laughed. "I suspect those two were near the top of the list of things that inspired Millie's retirement. She'll be delighted that *you* got to deal with them this year."

Julie nodded without answering, surprised to realize that it made her feel better.

"Oh, one more thing. I need to stay late tonight to use some of the books from the inn's library. I'm preparing a

new Stitches and Stories talk about pre–Civil War Straussberg."
Shirley's Stitches and Stories talks were a tradition at the Quilt
Haus Inn. Twice a week, the guests gathered in the formal dining
room and sat at the long table, busily working on projects,
while Shirley told stories from Straussberg's history. Julie had
sat in on a few and was surprised—and a little impressed—at
how much gossip Shirley could pack into her historical talks.

"That will be fine," Julie said. "Be sure to lock up on your
way out."

The remainder of the day continued at a bustling pace,
and Julie was relieved when she was finally able to retire to
her own small suite on the third floor. Her rooms were only
lightly furnished. All the pieces were antiques, but they showed
their wear even more than the breakfast room chairs. Julie
didn't mind. She liked living among things that felt well used
and loved, though the rocking chair where she sat creaked
nearly as much as the old wood floors.

She rolled her shoulders, acutely aware of the tension
that had built up over the day. There was no way she could
sleep while she was so stiff. She stood and began a series of
stretches. Some she had "borrowed" from yoga, and others
were just stretches she remembered from high school gym
class. Over the years, the stretches had become part of the
prep for every recovery job, loosening tension that could break
her focus. Of course, lack of focus at her present job wasn't
likely to land her in mortal danger. If she were honest—and
she tried always to be honest with herself—she was finding
the new job a little chafing. It wasn't boring. There was too
much work and too many crises to be boring. But she missed
the thrill of the hunt and the challenge of a good adventure.
And she loved the feeling of completion that came at the
end of a job.

At the inn, the job never ended.

She sighed softly as she kicked off her shoes. She needed to focus on her new life and stop pining for the one she'd left behind before it could kill her. She reached high over her head, her back slightly arched, and felt her muscles stretch from the demands she placed on them. That's what she needed to do—stretch and appreciate the new demands.

As she swung forward to reach for her toes, a sound in the hallway caught her attention. She froze. The clock on her small fireplace mantle made it clear the hour was much too late for a guest to be wandering around up here. She wondered for a moment if Hannah might be coming up to see her. Then she thought of Shirley. Perhaps Shirley had found something downstairs that needed Julie's attention, or a piece of juicy local gossip she had to share or she would burst. Julie raised herself to standing and waited for the knock at the door. No knock came.

Quietly, Julie crept to the door and opened it a crack. She saw that the door to the tower suite hung slightly open. It seemed Daniel Franklin had taken to wandering around at an unusually late hour.

I knew those blue eyes were trouble.

She slipped out of her room and tiptoed softly to his door. When she peeked in the open doorway, the room was empty. The beautiful brass bed was still neatly made. So why was their newest guest wandering around the inn instead of sleeping?

She padded barefoot down the smooth wood stairs to the second floor and glanced down the hallway. No sign of movement. Since she couldn't imagine Daniel visiting any of her other guests, she continued down to the first floor. She peeked into the tearoom. The pastry case was empty for the night, but the case's light was still on, bathing the room in enough light to be certain no one lurked inside.

Then she checked the small library located beside the tearoom. Shirley sat curled up in one of the darkly upholstered Queen Anne chairs next to the fireplace. She had half glasses perched on the end of her nose as she squinted at one of the leather-bound books about Missouri history. Julie backed up quietly without speaking. She didn't want Daniel to be alerted by any sound, and a shouted greeting from Shirley would certainly carry over half the downstairs.

She walked across the foyer toward the breakfast room. The light of a full moon poured through the tall windows that flanked one wall of the room, casting pools of light and shadow. But Julie saw nothing out of place as her gaze swept over the room—until she noticed the door marked "Staff Only."

It stood ajar.

Apparently Daniel was not only restless, he was visiting areas clearly marked as off limits to guests. She quickly jerked open the door and spotted Daniel crouched down in the hall outside the kitchen, poking at the padlock on the cellar door with a thick piece of wire. His head snapped toward her at the sound, his eyes wide in alarm.

Julie crossed her arms over her chest. "Would you like to tell me why you're practicing your lock-picking skills on my lock? Or shall I simply call the police?"

FOUR

Daniel scrambled to his feet and slipped the wire into the pocket of his dark hooded sweatshirt. "It's not how it looks."

Julie raised an eyebrow. "So you weren't picking the lock to the cellar?"

Daniel ran a hand through his dark brown hair, his gaze darting about as if looking for the answer in the shadows around Julie. "Um, no, that part is exactly how it looks. I meant that I wasn't trying to get into the cellar to steal anything."

"Good to know," Julie said. "So, what? You wanted to commune with the furnace?"

His face darkened. "You're not making this any easier."

"I wasn't aware I needed to make it easier. You're in a part of the inn clearly marked for staff only. And you were trying to pick a lock. I can't think of any way to make a place more obviously off limits than a bright shiny padlock. So tell me why I shouldn't call the police, or at least boot you out of the inn."

"You know why I'm here in Straussberg."

"I know why you *say* you're here. Forgive me if I'm less accepting of your word in the matter, especially now."

"I told you the truth about *The Grand Adventure*," Daniel said. "But, while I was researching the ship, I found some information that ties the wreck to this inn." He paused. "And ties this inn to the treasure."

"I can assure you, we aren't hiding a steamship in the cellar."

"If you'd care to listen instead of making smart remarks. ..."

"I enjoy doing both. I'm a multitasker."

Daniel folded his arms across his broad chest, then leaned

back against the wall. "Fine. While I was researching the history of *The Grand Adventure*, I found a letter from the steamship captain to his wife. He references a vital cargo hidden aboard the ship, a cargo that must be kept secret."

"Did he say what it was?"

Daniel shook his head. "It looked like very ordinary cargo to him, but the cargo's owner paid him a ridiculous amount of money to keep the items off the ship's manifest. The captain believed the cargo was more than it appeared."

"So you have no way of knowing what the cargo was."

"No." Daniel paused, eyeing her appraisingly, then continued. "But the captain wrote that he had carved information about the cargo into the wood beam he was carrying to his wife's sister in Kansas."

"A beam."

"It came from the sisters' childhood home in Virginia. The captain took it when the old house was destroyed in a fire. The beam apparently was untouched by the fire. He had the beam cut in two. Half he made into a fireplace mantel in his own home, and half he was carrying to Kansas for the sister."

"How sentimental of him."

Daniel ignored that remark. "In the letter, he tells his wife not to scold him for the carving. He tells her the sister can sand it out, but she might like to keep it, given her love of quilting."

"What does a wooden beam have to do with quilting?"

"I have no idea," Daniel said with a grin. "But I'm looking forward to finding out. At any rate, he wanted some record of the items onboard and who owned them."

"And you imagine something in our cellar will shed some light on this mystery beam?" Julie asked, her tone reflecting how little she considered that a likelihood.

"Actually, I think the beam is in the cellar." Before Julie could offer another remark, Daniel held up a hand and kept talking. "That beam was unearthed in 1886 on a piece of land that is now the Winkler farm. That's what originally put me on the trail of the ship here. The carving on the beam was described in the newspaper from the period as looking like some crude attempt at an artistic design. I believe it's actually some kind of code. I hope to know more when I see it."

"We're quite a few miles from the Winkler farm."

Daniel nodded. "According to the newspaper, the beam was gifted to Ebenezer Stark, the brother of the man who owned the land. Stark was in the process of building a mansion, and the brother thought using the beam would be some kind of good luck charm."

"A beam retrieved from a ship that sank?" Julie pursed her lips. "That doesn't sound all that lucky."

"It wasn't. Stark had it built into his new mansion, and it didn't prove to be much of a good luck charm, as his wife died soon after at a young age. Stark then squandered his fortune on travel, drink, and gambling. Stark Mansion later passed through several hands before ending up where it is today." He gestured around him. "*This* is Stark Mansion."

"If this beam was a good luck charm, why would he put it in the cellar?" Julie asked.

"I'm not certain where he put it, but I poked around all the rooms I could today and didn't find anything. None of the public rooms feature rough-hewn wood anywhere. And none of the guest rooms I peeked into did either." He turned to tap on the cellar door. "What better place for something so plain and unfinished than the cellar?"

Julie narrowed her eyes as she thought about it. She didn't remember seeing any beams like he described anywhere in the inn, but she'd spent very little time in the cellar. "I'll go down with you and search, but you cannot do anything that will damage the inn, no matter what we find."

The boyish grin that split Daniel's face was irritatingly disarming. "No problem. Let's go."

Julie held up one finger. "One more thing. I get to be part of the treasure hunt."

He frowned. "If I find anything that could be classified as treasure, it goes to a museum. My interest is the hunt."

Julie felt a little jolt of the same thrill she used to get whenever she took on a new recovery job. "Same as mine. I like the finding, not the keeping."

His intense gaze seemed to size her up. "Then you have a deal. I'll welcome the help."

"Let me get the keys." Julie walked down the hall to the kitchen. The huge key ring hung on one wall. Millie had always carried the keys around with her, but the jingling weight made Julie feel like the jailer in an old Western movie. She grabbed the ring and soon had the padlock open.

The cellar light switch was mounted in the hallway so no one had to grope in the darkness for it. Julie flipped the switch, then hung the open lock on the dangling latch. "Let's go find your treasure beam."

The low-wattage lights were widely spaced in the cellar and covered with dust. This made everything dim as they walked down the shaky steps. Hanging cobwebs made it clear that the efficient Inga didn't venture into the cellar very often—if ever. Julie winced at the soft, slippery feeling of thick dust under her bare feet.

The floor of the cellar was packed earth. Dampness made the floor chilly, and Julie hopped in place to try and keep the soles of her feet warm.

"Charming place," Daniel commented.

"We don't keep anything down here but the furnace and electrical panel," Julie said, trying to ignore the musty air she tasted with each word she spoke. She led the way around the perimeter of the room. It didn't take long. As she'd said, the only large thing in the cellar was the furnace.

A few wooden crates, most covered with patches of mold, lay on the floor near the furnace. Julie wrinkled her nose as she spotted them. "I need to get rid of those." She gave the crates a nudge with her toe and the one on the bottom burst apart, spilling out old newspapers. She jumped back, treading on the toes of Daniel's boots as she did. "Well, Millie seems to have her very own antique fire hazard."

Daniel didn't spare them so much as a glance. Instead, he backed away from her and studied the floor joists over their heads, then returned to the stairs and studied their underside where rough wooden shelves had been fitted into the space.

Julie used the time to examine the walls. Two of the cellar walls were brick with narrow windows high on the wall. The windows were so thick with grime, she couldn't imagine getting any of them open. On one of the brick walls, an old coal chute sloped steeply upward.

The other two walls were sheer rock, as if the cellar had been blasted instead of dug. She put a hand on the rock surface. It felt cold and slightly damp, the same as the floor. She didn't really know anything about cellar construction but wondered if something could be done about the dampness. It occurred to her that if the grouchy twin sisters she'd dealt with that morning ever saw the cellar, they'd probably sue poor Millie for exposure to all kinds of bad things. The cool, damp room even made Julie a bit uneasy about the kinds of things that might be thriving in the packed dirt, the walls, or the half-rotten wooden crates. The more she thought about it, the more she wondered if she wasn't feeling just a little short of breath.

"It's not down here." Daniel's voice boomed from the shadows beneath the stairs, causing Julie to jump.

To cover her unease, she spoke more roughly than she normally would have. "Well, I like a wild goose chase as much as the next person, but we should probably call it a night. I'm cold, and I need to get some sleep. I'm sure I'll have a whole new collection of guests' crises to deal with in the morning."

"I was *sure* the beam was in the inn," Daniel muttered, shaking his head. "Maybe it's in one of the guest rooms I haven't seen."

"It's not. I've seen them all," Julie said. "Several times. Nothing like that is up there. The fireplace mantels are all delicate and small. And there are no beams in the ceilings."

Daniel looked around, his eyes narrowed. "Maybe it's built into the construction of the inn. It could be a doorway header or some other structural element."

"I'm fairly certain you are not going to get permission from Millie to tear up the inn looking for a wooden beam that *might* be hidden behind the walls somewhere."

"I haven't seen the kitchen yet."

"You're welcome to look, but the kitchen is the one totally modern room in this building. There are no exposed beams. And, no, you can't pull any walls down in there either."

"If you don't mind my looking, I would appreciate it," he said. "Are there any outbuildings? Any other old structures on the property?"

She shook her head. Suddenly, a strange scraping noise came from the top of the stairs. They both froze, exchanging worried glances. Then the lights in the cellar went off, plunging them into inky darkness.

"This really is an interesting place," Daniel quipped. "Full of surprises."

Julie shushed him, quickly reaching out, feeling for the stair rail. When she found it, she used it to guide her to the bottom step and carefully climbed the stairs with one hand out in front of her. Finally her knuckles rapped the cellar door; she'd reached the top. She listened at the door, but heard no further sounds. Who else could be skulking around the cellar in the middle of the night, and why would anyone turn off the light?

She turned the cellar doorknob and pushed. The knob turned easily, but the door didn't open. Julie pushed harder, rattling the door. She groaned as she realized what had happened. Someone had slipped the hasp back in place and padlocked them inside the cellar. "Hey! I'm down here! Open the door!"

She pressed her ear to the door again but heard nothing.

"So we're locked in?" Daniel's deep voice came out of the darkness on the stairs behind her. She'd been making so much noise, she hadn't heard him climbing the steps. "I don't suppose you know of another way out of the cellar?"

Julie shook her head, even though she knew he couldn't see it in the total darkness. "We're stuck, and I don't have a clue as to how to get out of here."

FIVE

"Do you at least have some idea as to who locked us in here?" To Julie's surprise, Daniel's voice sounded almost amused.

"I expect it was Shirley," she said. "She runs the tea shop, and I know she was working late. Plus, she's helpful. And she doesn't hear very well. I made her promise to lock up before she left. Obviously she decided to be really thorough about it."

"Sounds like the perfect combination to get us trapped in the cellar."

Julie realized she could now see a dark blob of Daniel on the stairs. Apparently her eyes were adjusting to the dim light that crept in from the streetlamp outside the grimy cellar windows.

The shadowy figure that was Daniel leaned against the wall at the top of the stairs near Julie and sighed. "Fortunately, aside from searching for the beam, my schedule was clear this evening," he said. "You?"

"I'd planned on getting some sleep," Julie said, more than a little unnerved at being trapped in the dark with Daniel. Alone.

"So what do you propose we do?" Again, she was certain his voice held a tinge of laughter.

Julie slipped her cellphone out of her hip pocket and checked to see if she could get a signal in the cellar. She could. She started to call Hannah, but then she pictured her friend's smirk at Julie managing to get trapped in the cellar with the handsome historian. "I can call my cook to come and rescue us," she said. "But I'd like to be sure we can't get ourselves out first."

She saw the blob Daniel nod. "Pride, right?"

"I hate to wake her in the middle of the night."

"Yeah. I'd be embarrassed too."

She knew Daniel couldn't possibly see her in the dark cellar, so she stuck out her tongue at him. The childish action made her feel surprisingly better. "Let's just try to solve our own problem first."

"Sure."

Julie used a flashlight app on her phone to light the way down the cellar stairs. She crossed to the far brick wall and shone the light up at the small window.

"You're a lot smaller than me, lady, but you're not going to fit through that," Daniel said.

She turned to glare at him, swinging the light in his direction. "Don't call me 'lady.'"

"Sorry," he said. "But I don't know your name. You've yet to offer it."

"Oh. It's Julie Ellis." She swung the light back around toward the window, but she was certain Daniel was right. Even petite Hannah couldn't have gotten through the small window. The most Julie would be able to do was get really stuck.

"Looks like you'd best wake your cook."

"I'm not *done* yet." She swung the light toward the coal chute. In movies, people were always wiggling through coal chutes, so she assumed it must be bigger than the other window. The chute was brick and slanted away steeply. Julie held up the light, but she couldn't get a good look at the window beyond. "I could definitely fit up the chute."

"You'll get dirty," Daniel said mildly.

"I'm washable. Can you give me a boost?"

Daniel laced his fingers together, and Julie stepped

her bare foot into them. "Your foot's ice-cold."

"That's because I left my shoes upstairs when I went to investigate why a guest was skulking around the mansion in the middle of the night," she snapped.

Julie took a hopping step up and shoved herself into the coal chute. The sides were steeply slanted, but since Julie filled most of the chute, she could wedge herself in and get enough leverage to creep upward. The rough brick and mortar scraped wherever bare skin touched it.

Finally, she reached the top of the chute. The crowded space didn't allow her to use her flashlight app easily. She reached out to feel for the window, but where her fingers should have touched glass, she felt something much rougher. She wiggled and squirmed until she could reach her phone in her pocket, then pulled it out and turned it on. That's when she discovered the original window was broken. Shards of glass still hung in the frame. "Great," she muttered. "I could have slit a wrist."

Beyond the broken glass, the window was bricked over. Julie groaned, then began the painful crawl back down the chute. As she was wiggling out the end, she felt Daniel's hands on her waist. He lifted her out of the chute and set her on the floor.

"Can we make the call now?" he asked.

"No. I'll find my own way out of here if I have to tear the door off." Then an idea struck her.

Apparently it struck Daniel at the same moment, because she could see him grin by the light of the cellphone. "We can take the door off."

Julie nodded. "We just need something to pry the pins out of the hinges. Something with a blade."

She turned to look around the cellar. Daniel tapped her

on the shoulder and held up a heavy bladed knife.

"Gah!" she exclaimed and jumped back, causing the light to dance across the deadly blade. It was a knee-jerk reaction, a carryover from her previous line of work. "You walk around armed with that thing?"

He laughed. "Only when I'm having adventures. It folds up."

Daniel strode across the room like a man on a mission, and Julie hurried after him, willing her heartbeat to slow to normal. The space at the top of the stairs was tight, so Julie had to lean against his back to hold the cellphone light while he worked with the hinge pins.

"You know," he said, "this adventure is becoming more fun by the moment. I think we make a great team."

"Just get us out of here."

"Yes, ma'am."

Though encrusted grime had to be scraped away to pull the pins, at least they didn't have to deal with paint. Daniel managed to get all three hinge pins out with minimal muttering under his breath. By the time the second pin was out, Julie had to hold the door upright so that the last pin would slide out. When it did, Daniel wedged his knife into the crack between door and frame on the hinged side and began to lever it toward them.

The hasp groaned as they forced its small hinge to bend. Julie winced, wondering what damage she might be inflicting on the door. She would have to pay for any repairs since it was her pride that led to the damage.

Finally, Daniel was able to pull the door open a crack. "You're smaller than me; see if you can squeeze through. If you can, I'll rehang the door, and you can let me out the more traditional way."

"Don't sound so sure of yourself."

He merely chuckled.

Julie made it out. She briefly considered leaving Daniel in the cellar for the remainder of the night as punishment for all of the trouble he'd caused, but ultimately decided against it. Daniel worked quickly to replace the door pins, and he finished up about the same time Julie got the lock off and opened the door. She was relieved to see that the door wasn't damaged, though the latch was definitely bent.

"Well," Daniel said as he rubbed his hands on his well-worn jeans. "That was fun. Still OK if I take a peek in the kitchen?"

"I suppose." Julie walked the rest of the way down the hall, then used the cleanest spot she could find on her hands to push open the swinging kitchen door. Once in, she flipped on the lights.

Daniel glanced around, frowning. "They may well have covered it up in all this remodeling." He walked over to the tiny breakfast area where Millie sometimes held staff meetings when she was in town. Next to it was a small fireplace. It was considerably more rustic than the rest of the fireplaces and looked old. "This mantle is old, but there are no marks on it."

"Nope."

He continued to stare at the single thick piece of wood that made up the mantle. "What if Stark had the beam installed with the carving facing the wall? This *could* be it. We'd know for certain if we could dig it out of the wall and examine the other side."

"I'm afraid that's permission I can't give. And I'm almost one hundred percent certain Millie wouldn't go for it either. She's very fond of how this kitchen looks."

"Even if I promised to put it back exactly how I found it?"

The expression on his face was so hopeful that Julie felt bad for shaking her head. "No. Sorry."

"Then I guess we should call it a night," he said. "And what an interesting night it was. I appreciate your help. It was very gallant of you to try and climb out the coal chute to save us."

Julie studied his face, his teasing tone causing her eyes to narrow slightly. "And it was very brave of you to risk life and limb taking the pins out of the door. *Partner.*"

"Touché." He grinned and strode toward the main staircase, leaving her to watch his retreating form.

Julie gave herself a mental shake and reached up to turn off the lights. She caught sight of the kitchen clock as she did so and almost moaned. Morning was going to come far too soon.

She was right. The alarm clock in her room seemed to ring moments after she'd finally wound down enough to close her eyes. Her head felt mushy, and her eyes hurt. She wobbled to the small bathroom, hoping for some rejuvenation from the shower. It helped, but not a lot.

As soon as she reached the first floor, Julie headed for the kitchen. She definitely needed the cup of coffee she'd been fantasizing about since the scream of the alarm had woken her.

Hannah glanced up from the dough she was rolling out. "Wow. You look terrible. Insomnia?"

"Something like that." Julie shrugged. "I was treasure hunting in the cellar."

"The cellar ... here? The one with all kinds of nothing in it?"

"That very one." Julie picked out the strongest coffee pod in the basket and popped it into the machine. Then she tapped her foot as her mug filled. "We found all the treasure you'd expect."

"Why were you looking for treasure in the cellar?"

"Daniel Franklin felt certain it was there."

Hannah rubbed soft butter over the dough. "I knew he had to have a flaw. He's too handsome. Figures he'd be crazy too."

Julie sipped the hot coffee, then rubbed her forehead. "He said he read something about a rough wooden beam with a coded message carved into it. It supposedly ended up at the inn, but there's nothing like that in the cellar."

"Oh. Well, I'm not surprised it wasn't in the cellar since I know exactly where it is."

Julie blinked, her tired brain trying to follow the meaning of what she'd just heard. "You do?"

"It's the fireplace mantel in my bedroom," Hannah said, sprinkling the dough with cinnamon. "Servant quarters aren't as fancy as the rest of the house. Luckily, I kind of like the rustic look. I've puzzled over the carving a couple of times since we got here. I even looked online, but I haven't seen a design exactly like it."

The kitchen door swung open, and Inga Mehl walked in, looking as dour as always. Hannah began to roll up the dough and said, "You can start on the bacon, Inga."

Inga nodded, then turned to Julie. "I found something when I was sweeping the porch this morning."

Julie felt slightly chagrined. She wasn't aware Inga swept the porch in the mornings. The housekeeper's job was a lot like that. She moved through the house, quiet as a baleful ghost, and left cleanliness in her wake. "What did you find?"

Inga held out a scrap of cloth. "It was shoved into the crack between bricks on the base of one of the posts. There's a small gap where some of the mortar has come out."

Another thing that needs fixing, Julie thought as she took the scrap of fabric from Inga. The fabric was surprisingly clean for having been left outside. Someone had stitched a message on it in ornate red letters: "Treasure hunting can be a deadly endeavor … for the hunter."

A chill crept up Julie's back, and she fought the urge to fling the ominous scrap of cloth onto the floor. Why would someone spend so much time stitching a message like that? Was it related to Daniel's treasure hunting? That seemed unlikely. Daniel had only arrived the day before.

Julie's stomach clenched as she had another thought. Her work in antiquities recovery was a lot like treasure hunting. What if her past had already caught up with her, and this was the art theft ring's way of playing games before moving in for the kill?

Inga turned away, leaving Julie to stare at the cloth. Seemingly oblivious to Julie's turmoil, the housekeeper pulled a thick butcher-paper-wrapped package from the fridge and set about unwrapping it.

Julie cleared her throat nervously. "Inga, did you happen to see anyone out on the porch yesterday?"

Inga looked at her, expressionless. "No. But I wasn't outside often."

Julie nodded. "Thank you."

Julie felt Hannah's gaze on her. She looked at her friend, who raised an eyebrow.

"Do you still want to see the beam in my room?" Hannah asked.

Julie shook off her worry and crammed the cloth into her pocket. *One mystery at a time.* She forced a smile. "I do, but I don't want to interrupt your breakfast preparation."

"Just let me finish rolling these and pop them in the oven."

A short while later, they entered Hannah's quarters. The second they closed the door to the small sitting room, Hannah whirled and said, "Spill it. What did Inga give you?"

Julie showed her the scrap of fabric, and Hannah looked it over curiously. "Nice work. I couldn't do anything this nice. Maybe in cross stitch, but this looks like split stitch." She held the fabric close to her nose. "And I don't see any sign of marking on the fabric. I think this was done freehand. Wow, whoever did this really has talent."

"How lovely for them," Julie said dryly.

"Do you think this warning has something to do with the arrival of our new treasure hunter?" Hannah paused. "Or your old activities?"

Julie shrugged. "I don't know. And since I can't know for certain, I don't intend to worry about it." She held out her hand for a fabric. "So, where's the carving on the beam?" She looked around the neat room and headed for the fireplace.

Hannah pointed at the small strip of carving. The symbols were squares with odd marks making some of the squares different from the others. Julie ran her finger gently over the carving. Then she looked up and smiled. "Bingo!"

SIX

The wooden beam was dark with age, but the carefully carved squares were darker still. Julie leaned in to look closely at them, and she saw that they seemed to have been cut with a chisel rather than a knife. The edges were precise, and each gouge was a neat valley in the wood. "Someone went to a lot of trouble with this message too. Daniel's theory might be correct after all."

"If you don't mind," Hannah said, "I'd just as soon you didn't bring your new adventure partner in for a tour of my private rooms."

"No, of course not. Still, I'd like to make a rubbing of this. Maybe I can figure out what the symbols mean."

Hannah moved to the side table beside her brass bed. She pulled open a drawer and rummaged around until she found a package of tissue paper. "Do you think you can do a rubbing with this?" Hannah brought it over along with a red crayon.

"Crayons?" Julie asked.

"I have a bunch of them. I bought them to give to fussy kids in the breakfast room, but we don't really get kids in the breakfast room."

"Not a lot of quilting preschoolers," Julie said.

"I was trying to be thoroughly prepared for any possible emergency."

Julie peeled the wrapper off the crayon and laid the tissue paper over the carving on the beam. Then she rubbed the crayon gently against the paper. The lines of the carving appeared on the paper. Julie continued to rub the crayon until the carving was dark enough to easily read. "Got it."

"Great. It's time I got back to fixing breakfast."

"And time I got back to work." Julie folded the rubbing and slipped it into her pocket alongside the embroidered note. It had certainly been the morning for cryptic messages.

As soon as she reached the lobby, she found Daniel leaning back against the polished oak front desk, studying the quilts on the walls. He straightened when he saw Julie approach.

"There you are," he said with a warm smile. "I wanted to thank you for humoring me in my hunt for the elusive wood beam last night."

Julie couldn't suppress her own grin. "I have to admit it was a nice change from my usual adventures here." She fingered the rubbing in her pocket. She'd already decided against sharing it with him until she could spend a little time with it. She rather liked the idea of handing it over decoded.

"I'd imagine." He shoved his hands into the pockets of his jeans and looked uncomfortable for a moment.

"Is something wrong?"

"No, everything's fine."

"Did you want to ask me something?"

He looked up at her, and she admired the lovely pale blue-gray of his eyes. "Ah, no. I just wanted to say thanks. I'm heading over to the Winkler farm."

"I hope you have better luck today than you did last night." She fidgeted with the rubbing in her pocket, starting to feel a tiny bit guilty for withholding such an important clue. But not guilty enough to come clean.

"Thanks," he said, but he continued to stand at the front desk. Staring at her.

She began to fear that he *knew*. Folding her arms across her chest, she lifted her chin defiantly and waited for him to speak.

The awkward silence stretched almost to the breaking point before he finally spoke. "See you later." His words tumbled out in a rush.

Julie watched in bewilderment as he practically ran out of the inn. She could understand if *he* were the one with the coded message crammed in his pocket, but what could possibly be making him act so oddly? Whatever it was, Daniel Franklin had the worst poker face she'd ever seen.

Finally, she shrugged and returned her attention to the front desk. A cheerful couple came down the stairs and showered Julie with praise while they checked out.

"You're not staying for breakfast?" Julie asked.

"We have to get back on the road," the man said.

"We're on our honeymoon," his wife whispered, and her pale cheeks pinked as she spoke.

Julie looked at their nearly matching gray heads and smiled. "Congratulations."

"We've been married for thirty years," the man said.

"But we never had a honeymoon," his wife added. "So this year we decided to do it. Today we're driving on to Branson."

"That should be exciting," Julie said.

"We haven't been there since the kids were little," the lady said, lowering her voice as if she were revealing a secret. "And now we're going by ourselves."

Julie wished them well, feeling a nice glow from their happiness. The rest of the morning passed in its usual blend of joy and crisis. Another guest checked out after breakfast and also complimented everything about the inn. Then a different guest caught up with Julie after breakfast to say she was certain her room was haunted by a ghost scratching at the walls. When Julie examined the room, she saw mouse droppings in the closet. Julie put down live-catch traps and offered the woman a different room. The guest was clearly disappointed that she hadn't heard a ghost, but she accepted the change happily enough.

By late morning, most of the guests had either left the inn for the day to pursue their own activities or had settled into one of the comfortable public rooms for some quilting. Julie peeked in on the tearoom, where Shirley was having a little workshop on embroidery stitches. Julie was glad to see that most of the tearoom tables were filled.

With everything so quiet, she hopped up onto the stool behind the front desk and pulled out the rubbing from the mantel. She spread it out and studied the symbols. Each was a little box with dots and tiny marks along the edges. There was something vaguely familiar about the look of the row of boxes. The squares reminded her a little of the squares on a quilt, but beyond that she couldn't tell much.

She pulled out a second sheet of paper to copy the designs, thinking the process of drawing them might shake loose an idea. As she did, Mrs. Eddings, one of their most frequent repeat guests, stopped and looked at what Julie was doing.

"That's an interesting design," she said. "Are you planning quilt blocks?"

Julie looked up to smile at the thin woman's friendly curiosity. "Actually, I think it's a code, but I can't figure it out."

Mrs. Eddings lifted her reading glasses from where they dangled around her neck on a chain. She perched them on her nose and peered more closely at the papers. "It looks a little like the Masonic cipher, but not quite. There are no triangles, and none of the squares have open sides."

Julie looked at her in surprise. "You're right. That's why it looked vaguely familiar to me. But how did you recognize it so easily?"

The old woman chuckled. "I'm a retired schoolteacher. I taught American history, and the Masonic cipher was one of my kids' favorite things. Every year, all the notes slipped around in my class would be in code for a solid month after that lesson." Then she tapped the paper. "Still, that's not really the Masonic cipher, but it looks a lot like it." Then she shrugged. "Of course, they also look a little like the squares of a quilt."

Julie's eyes lit up. They did look like both squares on a quilt and the Masonic cipher. What if they were? The old ship's captain was sending the message to his wife and a woman of that period would certainly know quilts. Then she remembered the letter that the captain sent to his wife had mentioned her love of quilts. Was that a clue to how the cipher was laid out?

The original Masonic cipher was based on two tic-tac-toe boards and two crossed-line figures. One set of each had a dot in the middle of every square or triangle. So what if the captain did the same kind of pattern, but with three Nine-Patch quilt figures instead of the traditional form?

Julie quickly sketched out each Nine-Patch quilt. The cipher had been drawn with an X at the corners of the center square of each quilt, and they crossed into the corner of the adjacent squares. In addition, one of the Nine-Patch quilts had heart designs at the center of each block, while another had a dot in the center of each block. The third had nothing at the center of each block.

Once Julie had drawn out the quilt squares, all she had to do was figure out the order in which the quilts were laid out. Did the A square have a dot at the center, or a heart—or nothing? Once she knew that, she could tie the rest of the letters in the alphabet to a square and crack the code.

Mrs. Eddings looked over the drawings excitedly. "I think you have it! What a quick mind you have. Every square in each Nine-Patch quilt must be a letter—except one. That probably serves as a blank space to separate words. Figuring out which of these corner squares is probably the blank space should be a big help."

Julie laughed. Mrs. Eddings must have been a very encouraging teacher. "Can you help me work out the order of the three quilts?"

The old woman took Julie's place on the stool, and the two worked by trial and error to figure out the order, though Mrs. Eddings's thoughts about the blank space certainly shortened the job.

When they finally hit on the right order, Mrs. Eddings clapped her hands. "That was such fun! I still have no idea what the message is trying to tell you, but at least it's readable now."

"It is," Julie agreed as she stared at the papers. "Although I was hoping for something a little less obscure."

The old woman shrugged. "It's a nice little poem. Well, I really need to buy some thread. I got so caught up in this, I completely forgot what I'd come downstairs for."

Julie thanked her, then turned back to the message and sighed. Maybe it would make more sense to Daniel. She folded up the papers and slipped them back into her pocket. Then she turned to the far less entertaining job of working on the inn's finances.

When Daniel returned later in the day, Julie was dealing with another crisis. She could only nod as he waved in passing. The sisters had heard about the mouse at the other end of the hall from their room and were terrified that it was in the process of looking for them.

"Animals can sense when people are afraid," Mrs. Cantrell insisted. "They sense it, and they attack."

"You're concerned about being attacked by a mouse?" Julie asked.

Mrs. Cantrell narrowed her eyes. "They spread disease."

"Plus," her sister added, "I'm allergic."

"To mice?" Julie asked.

"To anything with fur."

"I'm not certain what you want me to do," Julie said helplessly. "I put out traps in the room where the mouse was. I could call around and find you a room at another inn."

Both women looked instantly affronted. "We don't want to move," Miss Lawson said.

"That's entirely too disruptive," her sister insisted. "We've already been moved once because of problems here. We simply want you to catch the mouse before we retire for the evening."

"Oh." Julie wasn't sure what to say to that. Catching a mouse wasn't exactly like tracking a bear. You had to wait for it to come out and end up in the trap. "Well, I've set the traps."

"What did you use for bait?" Mrs. Cantrell asked. "Peanut butter works best."

"No," Miss Lawson said. "Bacon works best. I've told you that a hundred times, Clarice. Bacon is far more effective than peanut butter. You're simply too cheap to bait the traps correctly."

Julie looked back and forth between the two women. "I used cheese."

"Cheese!" Miss Lawson was clearly horrified. "You can't catch a mouse with cheese. What kind of innkeeper puts cheese in a mouse trap? Anyone would think you'd learned about mice from cartoons."

The truth was, Julie *had* learned about mice from cartoons, but she chose not to mention that. She hadn't had to deal with mice getting into her apartment in New York.

After a few more minutes of the sisters' theatrics, Julie reluctantly agreed to rebait the traps. She even let the sisters follow her, clucking with disapproval, to the kitchen to look over the bacon and peanut butter options.

Hours later, Julie had finally managed to head off every impending disaster and retire to the peace of the third floor. She tapped on Daniel's door before heading to her own. He opened the door so quickly, she wondered if he'd been waiting for her. His smile was certainly warm and welcoming.

"I have something to show you," she said. "I found the beam."

His already cheerful expression bloomed into delight. "You did? I can't believe it! Where was it?"

"In our cook's room," Julie said as she pulled the papers out of her pocket. "I took a rubbing." She unfolded the thin paper and handed it over.

Daniel moved away from the door and stepped closer to the room's lamp to study the markings. "It looks almost like the Masonic cipher, but it's not."

"No, it's based on Nine-Patch quilt blocks," Julie said.

He looked up, and she was pleased to see she'd impressed him. "I don't suppose you figured out what is says?"

"With a little help from a guest," Julie admitted as she pulled the rest of the papers from her pocket and took a step inside the room. "But the message isn't exactly enlightening." She started to hand them over, then hesitated. "Don't forget, you promised to let me be involved in this treasure hunt."

"I won't forget," he said. "And I'm not likely to turn down anyone who wants to help. Let me see what you figured out here before I burst, and then I'll tell you all about my day."

Julie handed him the papers, and Daniel read the deciphered message aloud: "'Mey apples fill the finest crock and hew a space in Southern stock.'"

"Does that mean anything to you?" she asked.

"The words 'hew' and 'stock' could be a reference to a hiding spot for some of the treasure," he said. "It could be hidden in a compartment hewn into something. Maybe the stock of a gun?"

"Then the treasure would have to be very small."

"Could be jewels," he said. "There was a war coming, and some families sent their more portable valuables to family in the territories. This could be a case of that."

"But what about 'Mey apples'?" she asked.

He shook his head. "Once we find the ship, this might make more sense."

"So, tell me about your day."

Daniel gestured toward the room's cozy rocking chair. "Please, make yourself comfortable." He sat nearby on an ottoman. "I walked the Winkler property today, working out where the ship's most likely location could be. Tomorrow an old friend of mine will be meeting me at the farm. George is a geologist, and he's bringing a magnetometer to search for the wreckage through the ground."

"Is that like a metal detector?" she asked.

"A magnetometer identifies magnetic fields," Daniel said. "Any large deposits of iron will give off a strong reading."

Julie nodded. "Like the cast iron in a steamship boiler. Sounds interesting."

Daniel laughed. "It's not. I'll be following George around with this backpack magnetometer and listening to him sing badly, but you're welcome to come out. He'll like having a new audience."

"I don't mind a nice, peaceful morning out on a farm," she said. "I could use a little bit of boring after the last couple of days here."

"Well, it might not be totally quiet. I did call the local newspapers and television stations." Julie's expression must have reflected her dismay, because his tone turned apologetic. "I really need the publicity. If I can drum up interest, I won't need to finance everything myself. Right now, I can cover it as long as nothing goes wrong. But I've yet to see an excavation where nothing goes wrong."

"So you're looking for investors?"

"I will be," he said. "And it will be easier if I can get the word out."

She couldn't fault Daniel's reasoning, but that didn't mean she liked the idea of the media being at the search. Julie had been very careful to avoid getting her picture taken since moving to Straussberg. She didn't know how much energy a criminal art theft ring would put into tracking her down, but she was certain she wouldn't enjoy the result if they managed to do so.

Still, she didn't want to pass up a chance to be involved in the search for treasure. It felt like old times to have an adventure ahead of her. She'd just have to be sure she stayed clear of any photo ops. How difficult could that be?

SEVEN

By the next morning, Julie had nearly convinced herself that the search for a ship on dry land wasn't likely to draw any media interest at all. She kept telling herself that the only people she'd encounter at the farm would be George, Daniel, perhaps the owner … and no one else. No media. No cameras. The pep talk worked until she walked into the kitchen for her coffee.

The smell of fresh muffins hung in the air. Hannah pulled two pans from the oven and set them on cooling racks. "Have you seen the paper?"

Julie shook her head as she walked to the coffee maker. "Not without my coffee."

"Your boyfriend made the front page—under the fold, but still front page."

"I don't have a boyfriend." Julie picked up the newspaper from the counter. The *Straussberg Gazette* must have been having a slow news day because the headline read, "A Sunken Ship on Dry Land?" She skimmed the article and saw it consisted mostly of the same things Daniel had told her, only the writer had spun the story so that Daniel sounded like a deluded idiot.

"Have you considered that it might not be a good idea to have him at this inn?" Hannah asked as she shook the muffins out of the pans onto the racks.

Julie looked up. "Why?"

"Because you don't need the media interested in anything around you."

"The article doesn't mention the inn," Julie said. "Just Winkler Farm."

"Well, someone seems to know about treasure hunters at the inn," Hannah said. "Or have you forgotten the little hand-stitched love note someone left on our porch?"

Julie stiffened as realization dawned on her. "You know, I had half dismissed the possibility that the message was for Daniel because he'd only just arrived at the inn. But what if the note *was* meant for him? The more I think about it, stitching a threat onto cloth doesn't seem like the kind of threat a criminal art ring with ties to the mob would make."

Hannah carefully placed the warm muffins into cloth-lined baskets, then nodded. "You have a point. I envision the art ring sending you a bomb, or maybe a finger, but not a piece of stitchery—and a pretty one at that."

"It's possible the stitcher never imagined I would assume the message was addressed to me," Julie said. "If we weren't worried about the art ring, we would have been certain the threat was addressed to Daniel."

"Maybe you should ask him if he has a stalker. Though not this morning." Hannah pointed a muffin at Julie. "This morning you should stay as far away as possible from Winkler Farm and the media attention that's likely to be there."

Julie snatched the muffin out of Hannah's hand and took a bite. The burst of warm apple flavor was a welcome distraction from all the talk of gloom and doom. "I *have* to go to the farm. I practically extorted the invitation. Daniel will wonder why I changed my mind if I don't."

"Tell him there was an emergency here. If you give it a minute, there probably will be."

"No. I said I'd be there, and I will. Besides, I already have the morning scheduled to be off, so you're not getting out of crisis-management duty that easy. Shirley will be here to help, but you'll need to man the front desk."

"I wasn't trying to avoid work," Hannah said. "You need to take this risk seriously. Criminal mafia rings aren't known for their forgiving nature. You *stole* something from them. Something very valuable. Do you think they're going to let it go that easily?"

Julie didn't know how to make her friend understand that she *was* taking the risk seriously. She just wasn't willing to let it run her life.

"I'll be careful," Julie said. "Promise."

By the time she met Daniel in the lobby, she'd cleared up two small guest complaints and managed to snag another of Hannah's fantastic muffins. All in all, she considered it a good morning.

One look at Daniel's face, and she could tell it wasn't going quite as well for him. "Problems?"

"Did you see the newspaper?" he asked.

Julie nodded. "I thought you wanted publicity."

"I didn't want to be described as 'delusional.'"

"That's the thing about publicity. Once you let that tiger out of the cage, you can't do much to control it."

"I hope they man up and print some kind of retraction when we find the ship's location today." He looked around the lobby, and Julie followed his gaze. As always, the room was almost painfully clean. Sometimes Julie wondered if Inga were magic.

Daniel's next remark snapped Julie's focus back to the dig. "So are you free to go? My truck's parked close. It doesn't look like much, but I promise sitting in it won't get your jeans dirty."

"Not that I don't believe you," Julie said, "but I think I'd better follow you in my car. If there's a problem here, I'll have to come back before you're done."

The drive out to the Winkler farm was lovely. It made Julie realize she probably should make more of an effort to get out of the inn and look around the area. Recent rain had brightened the green grass, and the unusually warm fall had held off the frost. In the distance, the rolling hills were patched with shades of green as well.

Winkler Farm rested on surprisingly flat land, crisscrossed with barbed-wire fencing and dotted with outbuildings and a big white farmhouse off to one side. Julie turned onto the dirt road, where a sun-faded sign declared she'd find an organic farm stand within a half mile. Since Daniel continued on past the stand, Julie did little more than glance at the brightly painted wooden table piled with apples, pumpkins, and butternut squash. A slim woman in a dark green apron waved before turning back to attend to a customer.

They circled a long outbuilding with a blue metal roof, then drove past a muddy pond where brown cows with pink noses watched them balefully. Julie was never completely comfortable around farm animals. As a child, she had suspected they knew the farmer had evil designs and were only waiting for the right moment to take over the farm themselves.

The dirt road grew less and less well kept as they traveled away from the recently harvested fields. Eventually the road turned to little more than ruts, and Daniel rolled to a stop beside a boxy Mini Cooper. Julie eased in beside him, looking at the muddy ground suspiciously. She did not want to find herself stuck on the farm.

By the time she climbed out of her car, Daniel was a good twenty yards away, his long legs striding toward a red-haired man with a machine strapped to him and holding what looked like a white boom mike on a pole.

As Julie crossed the field, the red-haired man looked in

her direction, then said something to Daniel that made him laugh. By the time she'd reached them, the man she assumed to be George was almost bouncing up and down with excitement. "I'm so glad I don't have to spend the day with nothing lovely to look at!"

Julie raised an eyebrow. "The farm is beautiful."

George snorted. "The farm is a muddy rut with grumpy-looking cows, but *you* are a vision."

"Maybe you should have your vision checked," Julie said with a smile. "I'll assume you're Daniel's friend George."

"That's right," Daniel said. "George and I went to college together, but only one of us is still using the lines he learned there."

George laughed. "I learned all my best lines from my grandfather. Show some respect."

"Don't take him seriously; no one ever does," Daniel said. "And never encourage him."

"You really don't need to," George said. "I encourage myself." He turned a pointed look at Daniel. "You're not going to tell me this lovely lady's name?"

Daniel gestured from one to the other. "Julie Ellis, George Benning. Remember, you've been warned."

"I believe I can take care of myself." Julie turned an interested look toward the mechanism strapped to the geologist. "So this is a magnetometer?"

"A rather old one, but it'll do what we need here," George said. "Those old steamships had massive amounts of cast iron in the engine and boilers. If there's one under the ground, we'll find it."

"I'm certain of it," Daniel said. "Julie found the beam at the old Stark Mansion, and it had the coded message on it. Since the beam was originally found here, it's simply a matter of locating the rest of the ship here too."

"You don't need to convince me," George said cheerfully. He turned to Julie and grinned. "I don't suppose you'd care to assist me? You can help me carry around my equipment. It's all connected, so you'll need to walk really close to me."

Julie shook her head. "You seem to be doing just fine. I learned to keep my distance from wolves on my first trip to the zoo."

George laughed heartily before turning to Daniel. "I'm so glad you found this one." George turned back to Julie to launch into an explanation of how the pulse magnetometer worked to find the magnetic field given off by the iron. She was about to tell him she didn't know what half the words he was using meant when a van came rumbling along the dirt road toward them. A battered car followed closely behind.

"And the media arrives," George said.

Julie slunk to the opposite side of George while Daniel stepped forward to greet the bored cameraman and reporter from the local television station. The two men practically had "They made me come" written across their faces. Still, Daniel treated them with his usual warm friendliness.

His tone turned a bit cooler when the woman from the newspaper introduced herself. The woman was thin to the point of looking sickly, as though her high cheekbones might suddenly cut through the skin of her face if she showed too much expression. Her trendy clothes contrasted sharply with the rusty wreck she'd driven up in. Julie's eyes traveled down to the sleek black trousers with gold zippers on the ankles and the two-inch heels with gold metallic toes. Julie noted how the thin heels of the woman's shoes kept punching into the packed mud with every move she made, causing her to wobble. Julie imagined that probably drove the woman crazy.

Certainly her smile looked angry and mean.

The reporter took one look at Daniel's glower and chuckled. "I see you caught my story on the wreck in this morning's paper," she said.

Daniel regarded her coolly. "It wasn't much of a story."

"I'm certainly open to expanding on it," she said with a sly grin. "Feel free to impress me."

Daniel turned away and spoke to the other reporters. "Let's get this search started." He led them toward George and the magnetometer while Julie slunk back toward the vehicles to stay out of the camera line. She heard George cheerfully chatter on about his machine as he began working a grid, searching for signs of the ship. The morning crawled by while George searched and Julie dodged any potential photos.

The newspaper reporter only snapped a couple of photos of George and Daniel, paying Julie no attention whatsoever. That suited her just fine.

Eventually the television people gave up and left. Julie had to give them credit; they'd hung in longer than she expected, given the brief attention span of television news. She was finally able to relax a little at that point.

As the sun grew warmer, Julie pulled her dark curls into a messy ponytail to let the breeze from the river cool her neck. Antiquities recovery was definitely more interesting than treasure hunting. She began to regret the thick cotton sweater she'd worn with her jeans. But she refused to give up and go back to the inn after the big deal she'd made out of her interest in the hunt. She could almost picture both Daniel and Hannah laughing at her lack of patience.

The newspaper reporter seemed to be having a similar problem with patience. She'd wobbled back to lean on her car and make cellphone calls. She flicked dirt off her trousers and shoes while giving Daniel and George occasional glances.

George was the only person clearly having a good time. Periodically, he would burst into song, usually with lyrics he'd obviously come up with on the spot. The songs tended toward bawdy, and virtually all featured really bad puns. In an act of mental self-preservation, Julie had pointedly stopped listening after he belted out, "When you're down by the sea and an eel bites your knee, that's a moray!"

The sound of another car rumbling up the dirt road drew everyone's attention. It was a mud-splashed pickup truck. The driver looked like an advertisement for back-to-nature farming with his neatly trimmed blond beard and a cap advertising organic something or other. He ambled over to Daniel, nodding briefly at Julie. She assumed she was looking at the farm owner, Joseph Winkler, and her guess was confirmed on Daniel's first words.

"Joseph," he said, "have you met my friend George?"

The farmer nodded at George. "When he drove in."

Daniel pointed toward Julie. "That's my landlady, Julie Ellis."

From her periphery, Julie saw the reporter perk up minutely. She tensed, expecting the woman to move toward her. But apparently the "landlady" wasn't worth trudging through the mud for.

"Pleased to meet you," Joseph said, directing the polite words at Julie but then allowing his head to drift toward the reporter as well. He turned back toward Daniel. "I got a weird phone call and thought I ought to tell you."

"A phone call?"

"Some lawyer. I didn't recognize the name, though he says he's local. Anyway, he made an offer to buy my farm."

"I didn't know you were trying to sell."

"I'm not. Maddie and I love it here and an organic farm is our dream. The lawyer said he represented someone who didn't want to be named. They offered me a lot more for this place than it's worth."

"Why would someone do that?"

Joseph tipped back his cap to scratch his head. "That's the weirdest part of all. The sale was dependent on my stopping the search for the steamboat immediately. Now, we don't want to sell, so I'm not stopping you, but it's weird."

Daniel's face clouded darkly, and he folded his arms over his chest. "I'd sure like to know who would want to shut me down. As far as I know, I'm the only person in America who truly believes there's a steamship buried on this farm. Well, me and George."

George grinned at his friend. "Me? I'm just here for the beer afterward."

The farmer looked curiously at George's equipment. "Found anything yet?"

George shook his head. "But I still have a fair bit of the grid to cover."

Joseph nodded. "I should get back to the farm stand and help Maddie." He didn't move toward the truck but watched as George continued with his readings.

Suddenly, George let out a whoop. "I think I've got a live one!"

Daniel and Joseph crowded around him immediately. Julie hurried to join them. The numbers George rattled off didn't mean much to her.

"I don't really speak math," Julie said. "Did you find the ship?"

"Well, the readings aren't proof," George said. "But there's something big down there, and it's not natural."

Daniel bounced on his toes, grinning widely. "That's step one. We'll start drilling tests to map out the exact location of the hull, then we can start in earnest. We're on our way." He turned his grin toward the reporter, who was picking her way across the uneven ground. "So what do you think now?"

She shrugged and nodded toward George. "This guy is a friend of yours. This could all be something you made up to entice investors. Then you pocket the money and run."

"Pocket the money!" Daniel's voice rose. "I'm a respected historian, not a con man. I would never risk my professional reputation on a hoax."

The woman's smile was tight and cold. "That's not what I heard."

"Heard from whom?" Daniel stormed toward the reporter. She backed away. Julie was impressed to see the woman at least had some survival instinct.

"I don't reveal my sources," the woman snapped, though she kept backing up.

Daniel continued to follow her, shouting. "You need to be surer of your facts before you start spouting slander!"

The reporter tripped on something on the rough ground and fell onto her back. Julie smiled as she realized the woman seemed to have found a nice muddy spot to land.

Daniel held out a hand to help her up. "Are you all right?"

The reporter's voice rose to a howl as she ignored Daniel's hand and scrambled to her feet. "My clothes are ruined! Your aggressive behavior made me fall. You *are* crazy."

Julie shook her head as she walked closer. "Don't be absurd. The combination of inappropriate shoes and rough terrain made you fall." Then she stopped. Something was protruding sharply from the ground, and it didn't look like a rock. She knelt and touched the object. "Daniel, what's this?"

He dropped to his knees, ignoring the still-sputtering reporter. He dug into the damp ground, slowly scraping away enough mud to make one thing very clear. It wasn't a rock.

It was a bone.

"A bone!" the reporter shrieked. "This is a body dump site?"

"It's a little soon to jump to conclusions," Daniel said, still digging. George and Joseph quickly joined him, scraping away mud from the bone to reveal more and more of it.

"It looks like a thigh bone," Joseph said.

"Look at the size of that thing," the reporter said, her voice breathy with excitement as she snapped photos with her phone. "The man buried there must have been a giant!" She glanced at her watch, squealed, and ran for her car.

Daniel groaned. "Please tell me this isn't human remains. If we have to call in the authorities, I'll never get this dig going."

"I don't think it is," Joseph said. "As the lady pointed out, it's awfully long. I'm thinking horse or maybe a mule. I could call the vet who takes care of our cows. I bet he could tell you what animal it is."

"That would be fantastic. Thanks."

They finished uncovering the bone as they waited for the vet. When it was finally free, Julie had to admit, it looked like a leg bone to her. Not that she saw a lot of bones. The antiquities recovery profession wasn't *that* exciting. No one had ever hired her to recover human remains.

One thing she did notice in all the excitement: The mysterious offer on the farm was totally forgotten. But Julie suspected the offer might only be the first event. She looked across the wide farmland. Anyone who could throw around enough money to buy this place probably had other options for disrupting Daniel's work. The question that nagged at Julie was ... why? Why would anyone care about an old steamboat? She didn't have an answer, but she had a bad feeling about it. And her bad feelings were rarely wrong.

EIGHT

The Winkler farm quickly became the most talked-about piece of land in Straussberg, Missouri. Although the veterinarian declared that the bone came from a mule, the story about a "giant" buried on the Winkler farm had gone viral, along with the photo of the men digging it out of the mud. The photo could only have been taken by the reporter, but somehow she managed not to be linked to the bogus story online.

Every night when Julie finished handling the day's quota of crises, she climbed the stairs to her room, settled down with a cup of herbal tea that she made with an electric kettle, and waited. Sometimes she didn't even get through brewing the tea before the knock came at the door and a disheveled Daniel brought her stories of the treasure hunt.

One night about a week after finding the bone, Daniel accepted his own cup of herbal tea and sank into one of the chairs next to the small fireplace. He stretched out his long legs and tapped his toe against the fireplace tools, making them jangle lightly on their rack. "We finished mapping out the hull today," he said. "But we had to start digging a kind of well."

"A well?"

He nodded, then sipped at the tea, wincing slightly. Julie suspected Daniel didn't actually like herbal tea and drank it only to be companionable. "I ordered some big pumps. They should be in by the end of the week. We'll need to run them twenty-four hours a day to keep water out of the excavation once we really get started. We'll pump from the hole we dug today, like draining a well."

"Are you doing all right on money?" she asked as she settled into her own chair across from him.

He nodded. "My family was old money, and I'm the last in the line, so no one's around to complain about how I'm spending the family fortune. We'll make it. Though it would help if people lost interest in this whole 'giant bones' story."

"You're still getting giant hunters?"

He groaned. "Not as many, but the new batch is inventive. Some of them have been sneaking onto the site at night and doing their own digging. I've got stray holes all over, and now our machinery keeps breaking down. I suspect the giant hunters are messing with it at night. That's got to stop before my insurance carrier finds out and pulls the insurance for this little job."

"What are you going to do about it?"

He smiled. "George and I flipped a coin. He lost. So he'll be sleeping out at the site. We bought him a little pup tent and everything. You should have heard him complain."

"I'm surprised you're not taking turns."

He took another sip of tea, wincing again. "We will, but I won the toss, so I'm enjoying letting him worry about a long few months on a cot."

Julie looked pointedly at his mug. "You know, if you don't actually like herbal tea, you don't have to drink it on my account."

"It's growing on me," he said, taking another sip and smacking his lips. He pushed aside the paperback Julie had left on the small side table and set down the cup. Then he picked at a piece of cloth sticking out from under the book, finally pulling out the embroidered threat that Julie had completely forgotten about in the swirl of giant mania.

"What's this?" Daniel asked, holding up the scrap with a frown. "If you don't like my treasure hunt, you could have just told me. You didn't have to immortalize it in stitchery."

"Not my work," Julie said. "Our housekeeper found it shoved in a crack on the porch. I'd actually forgotten about it."

Daniel laid the scrap of cloth on his knee and studied it. "Nice work. Whoever did this is skilled."

"We *are* a quilter's inn. Many of the people here are skilled at that sort of thing."

"But why embroidery? I could think of much more threatening message forms, like blood on a wall or carving the words into an unfortunate murder victim."

Julie wrinkled her nose. "Aren't you gruesome!"

He grinned sheepishly. "I watched a lot of horror movies during my youth." He held up the cloth. "Do you mind if I keep this? I'd like to give it some more thought."

Julie wasn't enthusiastic about him keeping the note, considering she still wasn't certain it was for him. But she had no idea how to turn him down without spilling her own secrets. "Sure. It'll keep me from accidentally using it for a coaster. Don't lose it though, OK?"

He tucked it into the pocket of his worn flannel shirt, then patted it. "Safe and sound."

The next day, Julie turned down two different groups looking for a room. They clearly weren't quilters or stitchers, or people with any interest in crafting. She'd begun giving little stitching quizzes after she'd accidentally rented a room to one woman who came down to breakfast each morning wearing a UFO T-shirt and bothering the other guests with questions about local genetic anomalies and lights in the sky. Daniel wasn't the only one who would be glad when the giant craze died down.

After polishing off a dinner of apple-and-butternut-squash soup and fresh bread, Hannah and Julie wandered into the formal dining room, where Shirley was hosting her weekly Stitches and Stories event. Every chair in the room was taken. A few people leaned against the walls, listening avidly. To Julie's surprise, she realized one of the people was Inga Mehl. Her housekeeper's dark clothes lent her a chameleon air in the corner near the narrow servant's door. Inga was listening intently to Shirley, but the look on her face said she didn't like anything she heard.

Julie never screened Shirley's stories. Millie had told her to simply let Shirley "do her thing." The ones she'd listened to mostly wove together sketchy local history, ancient scandals, and quilting or other traditional crafts.

At the end of the long dining table, Shirley stood waving her arms dramatically as she spoke. Her hair clearly had been recently touched up, as the red almost seemed to glow. It surrounded her head like a corona, making her small round face seem like the smiling center of a child's drawing of the sun. Shirley's black quilted jacket was spotted with appliqués of the moon and sun and stars in various bright colors. She'd coupled the jacket with a sweeping broomstick skirt that gave her a faintly gypsy air.

Julie leaned against the doorway and listened. Shirley regaled the group with stories of unusual "goings on" around the area during the pre–Civil War era. Goings on that might be linked to "the Straussberg Giant." Julie noticed the ties to historical fact were looser than usual.

"Fur trapping was an essential part of Missouri history," Shirley said. "But the trappers weren't always too particular about what kind of critter they skinned. Some may have been cousin to Bigfoot. Bigfoot would certainly have giant bones."

No wonder interest in the giant bone wasn't dying down—there were too many people keeping it stirred up. She looked around the room. Most of the listeners were so caught up in Shirley's storytelling that they forgot to work on the quilting projects in front of them. One woman held her needle suspended in the air the whole time Julie watched her.

Julie switched her focus to the other guests. Some of them she didn't recognize at all, and she'd registered every guest at the inn. She did a quick head count. Not counting Inga, there were two more heads than there were guests. Plus, she didn't see Mrs. Eddings at all, so that meant there were at least three people in the audience who weren't guests.

One of the strangers held up her hand, then spoke. "What about the UFO sightings all over the state? I heard one pastor was called to pray over bodies in a UFO crash. Maybe that bone came from that crash."

Julie stepped into the room and edged around to see the speaker. It was the genetic anomalies woman. She was sporting a bright green T-shirt with "MUFON" printed on the front. The green wasn't a good choice with the woman's yellow-gray hair.

"There are simply more questions than answers," Shirley said, in a conspiratorial tone.

"Shirley," Julie said. "Can we chat after you wrap up here?"

Shirley offered her a bright smile. "Sure. In the kitchen?"

"That would be good."

Julie noticed the non-guests in the group turned especially

curious eyes toward her, so she slipped out quickly. It wasn't that she was scared of the stranger elements of Shirley's audience, but she'd rather not have them fixated on her.

When Julie reached the kitchen, she found Hannah perched on a stool with her laptop on the counter. "Isn't the little desk in your room more comfortable?" Julie asked.

"Probably," Hannah said. "But I like the kitchen. It's brighter and closer to the food."

Julie nodded. "Speaking of food, I want to eat something indulgent and full of calories."

"There are day-old chocolate croissants in the square plastic box in the fridge. I plan to make fresh cream cheese croissants for the tearoom tomorrow, so have fun."

Julie pulled the lid off the container, and the smell of chocolate and butter felt like a kiss to her senses. She took a huge bite of one, plopped the rest of the pastry onto a plate, and went looking for coffee.

"What's wrong?"

"What makes you think something's wrong?" Julie asked.

"Sweets binging after dark," Hannah said. "Classic Julie Ellis stress behavior."

Julie took another bite of pastry and mumbled around it. "I'm just hungry."

"Goody, a guessing game." Hannah grinned slyly. "Daniel?"

Julie shook her head.

"A guest?" Hannah looked pained. "Don't tell me the sisters are back. Those two kept sneaking recipes into my apron pocket the entire duration of their stay. Recipes for things I already do very well, thank you."

"Not the sisters." Julie sighed. "Shirley is giving Straussberg Giant theories in the dining room quilt talks."

Hannah laughed far longer than the news deserved in Julie's opinion. Finally her friend got a grip on herself and spoke though giggles. "I'm sorry. I'm just picturing this giant with an itty-bitty quilting hoop. How could she possibly tie this imaginary giant into quilting?"

"She isn't. It's basically all about giants—well, with a dash of Bigfoot and aliens."

Hannah chuckled again. "It keeps getting better."

"That's not better. I'm trying to keep the giant nuts out of the inn, and Shirley is giving talks designed to draw them back in."

"So tell her not to."

"Millie said Shirley has free reign with her talks. Apparently they're a big draw for the inn."

"I do what I can." Shirley's cheerful voice drifted from the kitchen doorway.

"The giant, Shirley? Really?" Julie said. "You know the veterinarian identified that bone as belonging to a mule. And Daniel said there was a mule tied up on the deck of *The Grand Adventure* when the steamship went down. Apparently the mule was the only casualty."

"That handsome devil would say whatever he had to if it meant keeping the excavation going. Plus, I never trusted that young vet," Shirley said. "I think he gets together with Joseph and smokes those funny mushrooms."

Julie heard a choking sound behind her that she recognized as Hannah trying to hold off another laughing fit. "I don't think they smoke mushrooms."

"I don't know what they smoke." Shirley waved a dismissive hand. "Or what Joseph Winkler grows. He's one of those hippy, back-to-nature types. You never know about those people."

"He's merely an organic farmer," Julie said. "And that's not the point. Some of the people in your audience tonight weren't even quilters. I recognized that UFO nut who spent three days here last week before I managed to move her to a different inn."

"I'm not sure that keeping an open mind is nutty," Shirley said with a sniff. "Besides, my Stitches and Stories events have always been open to the public. Millie established that rule herself."

Julie sighed. "I don't want to keep people out of your talk. I only wish you'd make the talk a tiny bit more quilting related."

"But this is important," Shirley said. "People are trying to cover up the secret of the Straussberg Giant just like they covered up the Cardiff Giant in New York."

Julie stared at Shirley for a moment without speaking. Finally she took a deep breath and said, "The Cardiff Giant is one of the biggest hoaxes in history. Right up there with the Fiji mermaid."

"*Hoax* is simply another word for successful cover-up!"

Julie shook her head. "Please. I'm begging you. Go with something related to quilting somehow for the next talk. OK?"

"Well, I'll have to do some research," Shirley said.

"Good. And maybe you could employ more reputable research sources."

"My research is impeccable."

"Really? And it led you to Bigfoot?"

"I go where the information takes me." Shirley pursed her lips, spun on her heel, and marched toward the swinging door.

It nearly hit her in the nose as Inga burst in. The

housekeeper came to an abrupt stop and looked around the room. "Excuse me. I didn't know you were having a meeting." She held up two teacups and a handful of napkins. "I cleaned up the dining room."

"Thank you," Julie said. "It could have waited until morning. You didn't need to stay late."

The look of shock on Inga's face almost made Julie laugh. "Shirley's *audience* had food in there. I couldn't let that wait for morning."

"Speaking of my audience," Shirley said. "Don't think I didn't feel you staring disapprovingly over my shoulder the whole time."

Inga frowned at her. "The topic was unseemly. This is a quiet retreat for quilters."

"Not all quilters like quiet," Shirley countered.

The other woman sighed deeply. "Apparently not." Then she managed a tiny quirking of the corner of her mouth. "Your hair looks lovely."

"Really? Thanks." Shirley patted the red cloud around her head. "I did it myself. You know, I could do yours."

Again Inga looked aghast. "I think not. But thank you." She looked down at the objects in her hands again, then quickly threw away the trash and put the china in the dishwasher. "I'll be leaving now."

"I'll walk out with you."

As the two left the room, Hannah whistled low under her breath. "You ever wonder how those two could be friends?"

"I try not to." Julie looked bleakly at her empty dish. "I'm going to need another croissant."

The next morning, Julie expected the cold shoulder from Shirley, but the tearoom hostess was as friendly as ever.

"You'll be happy to know I did some more research before

bed last night. I have a lead for my next Stitches and Stories," Shirley said. "And there are *no* giants involved at all."

"That's wonderful." Julie felt a rush of relief. She'd never believed it would be so easy to turn Shirley's attention to a different topic.

"Yes," Shirley said. "I spent some time on a few message boards. You'd be amazed what you can find online. I have a lead on a story about Missouri River pirates. They just might be responsible for that wrecked steamship!"

"I don't suppose there's any quilt information related to that."

"I don't know. But I read about some rich runaway wife from Louisiana right about the start of the Civil War. She might have been a quilter. The things I read didn't say, but some folks think she could have ridden on a steamship up the Missouri to get away with her lover. She was never heard from again." Shirley lowered her voice. "I think the pirates got her."

"How interesting," Julie said. She tried to look at the situation with a positive attitude. At least Shirley wasn't talking about giants.

"I found another post where someone with historical knowledge was talking about the possible cargo on the steamship," Shirley said and leaned in closer. "Swamp ape pelts."

"Swamp apes?"

"Bigfoot of the swamps. They're huge."

"Right." Julie had a sinking feeling that none of Shirley's new ideas were going to do much to cut back on people sneaking off to dig on the Winkler land. Before she could come up with a new—and likely desperate—plan to divert Shirley's attention away from the steamship, she saw the front door open. The woman who walked in exuded money and power, from the pointed toes of her high-end shoes to the tips of her short gray hair.

"May I help you?" Julie asked as Shirley scampered off to the tearoom.

"I hope so," the woman said. Her voice was soft, almost hesitant. She smiled and her eyes warmed. "I'm searching for possible locations to hold a fundraiser for my husband."

"A fundraiser?"

"Yes. I'm Alicia Parson. My husband is State Senator Walter Parson. We intend to hold a local fundraiser for his re-election campaign."

"Isn't Straussberg a bit out of the way?" Julie asked.

"Not to me. I adore Missouri wine country," Mrs. Parson said, her voice raising slightly from its soft tones as enthusiasm colored her speech. "My husband and I honeymooned here."

"Here in Straussberg?"

"Here in the Quilt Haus Inn."

Julie knew Millie would be excited to have the state senator's event at the inn, but she wondered where they could put everyone. The formal dining room was too small, and the breakfast room was larger, but rather homespun for the kind of event the cultured woman in front of her would surely want. She smiled at the senator's wife. "That's wonderful. I take it you're a quilter?"

"Oh yes," Mrs. Parson said. "I love quilting. My mother was a quilter and her mother before her. It's a wonderful way to feel connected to the women who fill the pages of this country's history." Then she sighed. "Unfortunately, I have so little time for it these days." She gestured toward the quilts hanging on the walls. "Just looking at the beautiful things you have here makes me want to take up a needle again."

"We're small here," Julie said hesitantly. "But if you feel we'd meet your needs. ..."

"I have some other venues to look at," she said, then she turned her sweet, warm smile on Julie again. "But this one is definitely my favorite."

"I know the owner will be honored that you even considered us," Julie said.

Mrs. Parson murmured a few other kind remarks about the inn and her memories of it. Then she asked, "Do you suppose you could put together a price list for my husband's campaign manager? Be sure to include availability dates."

"I'll be glad to," Julie said. "Perhaps you'd like to have a cup of tea in our tearoom while I type that up for you?"

"That would be very kind." Mrs. Parson turned to walk toward the tearoom.

To Julie's surprise, Inga Mehl intercepted the senator's wife before she got to the door of the tearoom. Inga's thick hair was pulled back so tightly that her eyes seemed to slant. The housekeeper wore her usual self-imposed uniform of gray skirt, white blouse, and shapeless gray cardigan, but her face was positively pink as she spoke.

"Mrs. Parson, I wanted to tell you how much I admire the senator. He's doing a wonderful job."

Mrs. Parson's smile grew. "Thank you. I'm always glad to hear that."

Inga blushed and stammered another sentence about her admiration, then practically ran out of the room. Julie stared after her, wondering what on earth had happened to their normally hostile housekeeper.

"Your husband must be *truly* amazing," Julie said to Mrs. Parson.

The senator's wife chuckled lightly. "He has his days."

NINE

The glimpse of her housekeeper as a blushing fangirl proved to be the most unusual part of Julie's workday. No one tried to sneak in with UFO tracking gear. No one passed her any threatening needlework "notes." No one even demanded a new room at the inn. All the problems were completely run-of-the-mill. Julie found it a welcome change and made a silent promise not to complain about being bored anytime soon.

She was sipping her nightly herbal tea with her feet propped up on an antique tufted footstool when she heard the light tap on the door. She opened it to find Daniel standing in the hall, his hair damp and his feet bare.

"I decided to shower first," he said. "I was wearing more mud than clothes."

She looked down at his wiggling toes. "Then I appreciate the effort."

As Daniel settled into his customary chair, Julie put a fresh kettle on. She liked the routine they'd settled into. The truth was, she enjoyed spending time with Daniel. "Are you still working under the watchful eye of the giant hunters?"

"They've thinned down a bit," he said. "Though we're still getting night visitors. George sleeps like a log, though I haven't been able to catch anyone either. I suppose I shouldn't criticize."

"Must be frustrating."

He took the cup of tea she handed him and sipped it. "We were getting a little low on morale." He tipped a smile in her direction. "Until today."

She raised her eyebrows in question.

His white smile broadened to a grin. "We unearthed the first bit of the wreck itself today. It won't be long now before we begin bringing up cargo. We may even find something tomorrow."

They chattered on about the dig, but Julie noticed Daniel sneaking frequent glances at his phone.

"If you need to be somewhere, you don't have to entertain me," she said.

"It's not that. George and I were supposed to meet for dinner in town, but he never showed."

"And I'll assume he never called to tell you why."

Daniel nodded. "Not showing isn't really unusual. He was excited about something to do with the mud we were bringing up with the digger. When George is caught up in a geological wonder, he'll forget there's a world around him, but I did think he'd call eventually to tell me what kept him. It's too dark to be playing in the dirt now."

"Maybe you should call him?"

"I did, but he's not answering."

"And you're worried."

"Maybe a little."

Julie assumed that meant he was very worried but didn't want to admit it. "Why don't we drive out to the farm right now? You can show me whatever you've uncovered, and we can check on George at the same time."

"I'm not sure the mud-covered paddle wheel will be very exciting in the dark, but I'll take you up on it anyway. Let me get my shoes."

Once they arrived at the farm, Julie was reminded again of how incredibly dark night could be in the country. In the city, she sometimes had to search for shadowy places to hide when she was on a job. In the country, she could have carried off a calf and no one would have seen her, especially on a cloudy night like the one they faced as they bumped along the dirt lane in Daniel's truck.

"When we see George, pretend we came out here to show you the dig site," Daniel said. "I don't need to be called mother hen for the next month."

"Your secret is safe with me," Julie said, then added a soft cluck just to make him laugh. She leaned forward to peer out the truck window. "You know, you might have fewer prowlers around the site if you kept some lights on."

"We usually do," Daniel said. "I don't know why we're not seeing them yet."

Finally they ran out of dirt road. He shut off the truck's headlights for a minute, and they peered out at the uninterrupted blackness of the night. "There's no good reason for George to shut off those lights."

Daniel turned the truck's headlights back on so they could see to approach the dig site. He carried a long, heavy flashlight as well. "Stick close to me," he said. "The ground is a mess, between the big machines gouging up the mud and the gawkers tracking it around everywhere."

Julie didn't answer, though she had no intention of wandering far from the flashlight's beam.

"Someone has turned off the pumps," he said.

"Why?"

He shook his head. "I have no idea." When they got close to the excavation, Daniel darted his flashlight beam into the hole, and the light reflected back from the murky water. "Terrific. We'll have to run them all day to clear the water enough to be able to dig tomorrow. George would never have let anyone do that." He turned in a slow circle and shouted his friend's name. He got no answer.

Daniel walked carefully around the dig hole. They found uprooted stakes and two work lights with the glass broken out. "Vandals. Like we don't have enough trouble." Again he shouted his friend's name to no avail. "I don't like this."

"Try his phone," Julie said. "If someone knocked him out, he could be lying anywhere beyond the flashlight beam."

As soon as Daniel had punched in his friend's number, they heard a ringtone in the darkness. Despite her worry, a smile tugged at Julie's lips as she recognized the theme song from *Indiana Jones*.

They followed the ringtone to a point some distance from the dig and found the phone half buried in a clump of frost-wilted grass.

"You know," Julie said hesitantly, "the phone could have fallen out of George's pocket if someone knocked him out and dragged him."

Daniel stared into the darkness between them and the distant river. "I hope that's not the case, but I'm calling the police. None of this looks good."

While they waited for the police to arrive, Daniel checked on the pumps. It turned out they hadn't been vandalized, merely shut off. He started to flip the switch to turn the pumps back on when Julie put a hand on his arm. "You probably shouldn't mess with anything until the police get here. They'll want to see it all the way we found it."

He turned worried eyes toward her. "You think something bad has happened to George?"

"Don't you?"

"I don't want to. I want to think he lost his phone and went off to a late supper." Daniel clenched his fist in frustration. "I want his car to come rumbling down that dirt road right now."

"Maybe it will." Julie couldn't infuse enough enthusiasm in her tone to make it sound like she believed that.

In the dark, it was difficult to sense the passing of time. When the chilly breeze touched Julie's face, it smelled of a combination of mud and autumn. In the weeks since Daniel had come to Straussberg, autumn had crept in with Julie barely noticing. She'd grown used to the historian and his excitement about the dig. Now she felt the worry and tension emanating off him.

Finally lights appeared on the dirt road, but it wasn't George—it was the police. Julie was impressed with the efficiency with which they asked questions and began setting up lights to search the area. The truth was, she hadn't expected the officers to be so professional since they were from the slower pace of the Missouri wine country. But she'd been very wrong. She scolded herself for being such a city girl.

Daniel showed a policeman where he'd found the phone. "You don't suppose he dropped it there when someone attacked him?"

The officer set a marker in the mud where Daniel directed. "I don't see any blood or sign of a struggle here, so if he was attacked, I don't think this was the spot."

A sudden shout from the excavation site drew their attention. One of the officers was shining a light into the excavation hole itself. Daniel reached the edge of the hole before Julie and shouted George's name, his voice thick with grief and shock. Julie caught a glimpse of a body floating in the muddy water before officers herded both Daniel and her away from the edge.

Everything became a blur of action then as George's lifeless body was recovered from the hole and sent off in an ambulance. Julie watched the rush of movement, but with the dark pressing at the edge of all the portable lights, it all seemed unreal. Why would anyone hurt George? He was such a nice, cheerful guy.

She brushed her cheek and realized she was crying. She wiped the tears away, then looked down at her damp fingers. Julie Ellis *didn't* cry. She wrote it off to exhaustion and shock. She had seen a lot of rough scenes in her life, but this was her first murder, and it was someone she liked. Her attention sharpened as she heard Daniel raise his voice to a man in a rumpled suit. She drifted toward the conversation.

"You can't think I had anything to do with George's death," Daniel said. "He was my best friend!"

"And you had no disagreements?" the man asked blandly. Julie realized he must be a police detective. She eased a bit closer, careful not to catch his eye.

"Everyone has disagreements."

The detective looked up from making his notes. "That sounds like yes."

Daniel shook his head. "It shouldn't. George sang while he worked." Daniel managed a single chuckle while he thought about it. "He made up his own lyrics, and they were always terrible and distracting. So I complained, but it was half-hearted. Truth is, I always wanted to hear what nonsense he would come up with next." At that, Daniel's face seemed to slip, as if the skin had suddenly grown tired. His eyes looked dark and hollow in the artificial light. "I don't know why anyone would want to kill George."

The detective nodded, though Julie didn't see a speck of sympathy on his face. "These questions are just routine. Can anyone confirm when you left Winkler Farm this evening?"

"Maddie maybe," Daniel said. "She was cleaning up the farm stand, and I waved as I drove out."

"Maddie Winkler?"

Daniel nodded.

The detective continued to ask more and more questions, and none of them sounded routine. Suspicion rolled off the man like fog from the river. He clearly believed Daniel had killed his friend. He was merely trying to work out why.

Julie walked over to the two men. "Did George drown?"

The detective's gaze turned to her sharply. "And you are …?"

Stupid, Julie thought. She did not need this man's attention. "I'm the innkeeper at the Quilt Haus Inn. Mr. Franklin is staying at the inn. And *you* are …?"

"Detective Frost." He cocked his head, like a hawk eyeing his prey. "Do you visit farms in the dark with all your lodgers?"

"That *would* be an odd activity," Julie answered with a nervous laugh. "Though I'd like to think any of my guests could count on me in an emergency. They're all away from home, after all. That's what lodging at an inn usually means."

"Was George Benning staying at your inn too?"

Julie shook her head. "He was staying out here at the farm. There had been incidents, vandalism on the dig site."

"And you knew this because?"

"Mr. Franklin told me." Then Julie smiled tightly. "Though he's not the only one I heard it from. Straussberg is a small community and very friendly. That can translate into everyone knowing your business, as you are probably aware, Detective Frost."

He dipped his head slightly in acknowledgement of what she said. Then he turned to look at Daniel again. "I'll have more questions when I hear back from the coroner. You'll need to stay in Straussberg for the duration of the investigation."

"I don't plan to go anywhere. My excavation is here."

The detective nodded. "We will, of course, need to secure this site while we investigate."

"I assumed that would be the case," Daniel said. "And I hope you plan to extend your list of suspects beyond me. Someone killed my friend. I hope you'll look long and hard to find out who."

The detective kept his steely gaze firmly on Daniel. "I will find the killer." Though he didn't say anything more, Julie could practically hear the words in the man's head. He believed he'd already found the killer, and he believed it was Daniel Franklin.

TEN

After being up half the night at the dig site, Julie slept through her alarm in the morning. She woke in a panic and didn't even take time to tame her curls before heading downstairs. She found Shirley at the front desk, beaming at her. The cheerful woman's cloud of red hair was covered with a bright blue crocheted cap that matched the bluebirds appliquéd onto her quilted jacket. "Hannah asked me to watch things a bit."

Julie made a silent promise to get something nice for her best friend as she thanked Shirley. "Did you have any problems?"

Shirley shook her head. "No one checked in or out." Then she leaned closer to whisper. "I heard about the horrible goings-on out at the Winkler farm."

"What did you hear?" Julie asked, dreading the reply.

"That historian fella went crazy and killed his friend."

"He did not!" Shirley's shocked face suggested Julie had snapped a little harshly. She softened her tone. "Mr. Franklin was away from the site when Mr. Benning died."

"Oh," Shirley said, disappointment clouding her features. "But someone *did* kill him?"

"The police didn't say. George was found in a flooded excavation hole in the pitch dark. It's possible he simply fell in. The mud is so slick, he might not have been able to get back out." Julie didn't think for a moment that's what had happened, but if she was going to have the hub of the gossip network working for her, she might as well use the woman to quell the more lurid rumors.

"Oh, how horrible." Shirley's round eyes made it clear she was imagining the struggle herself.

"I'm sure the police will figure it out eventually."

The front door opened and a short, round woman with close-cropped gray hair walked in leading a rolling suitcase like a dog on a leash. She was followed by a much taller man who looked around at the hanging quilts with the misery of someone who isn't looking forward to the next few days. As Shirley scampered back to the tearoom, Julie turned a warm smile toward the new guests, welcoming them to the Quilt Haus Inn.

Julie's morning quickly filled with the normal requirements of her job, but her focus kept straying back to that dark hole on the Winkler farm. With George dead, the mysterious call to buy the farm took on an ominous tinge. She would love the chance to look around the excavation site in the daytime, but she knew better than to tromp around a crime scene—especially in broad daylight. She wanted the police to look beyond Daniel for the murderer, but she'd rather they didn't look at her.

When she finally took a break to grab a sandwich in the kitchen, she was surprised to find Daniel chatting with Hannah while she showed him how to make *kuchen*, a cross between a small cake and a tart that was very popular in the tearoom. They both wore long white baker's aprons with "Quilt Haus Inn" stenciled on the bib.

"You know this part of the inn isn't public," Julie said.

Daniel gestured with the apple peeler. "I know. I'm hiding. Since I can't go out to the site, I'm stuck for something to do. I tried reading some local history in your library. You have quite a nice collection, by the way. But the lady from the tearoom kept popping into the library and staring at me."

Hannah cut a ball of pastry dough into small sections and began pressing them into tart pans. "Shirley's the curious sort."

Julie spotted a batch of huge chocolate chip cookies cooling on a wire rack and grabbed one. "I didn't know you were interested in baking."

Daniel shrugged as he set aside the peeled apple and picked up another. "I'm interested in everything. Besides, I've never been good at not working."

"I did think of something we might do." Julie bit into the warm cookie. The chips were still slightly soft and spread like silk over her tongue. She refrained from moaning. She didn't want Daniel to get the wrong idea.

"What?"

"I think we need to find out more about the person who made the offer to buy the farm," Julie said. "That was really the beginning of all the problems at the dig. I think if we find that person, we'll find someone new for the police to look at for George's death."

As Daniel peeled long green strips from the apple, he nodded. "Sounds like a reasonable idea, but Joseph said the lawyer didn't give the name of his client."

"No, but that can possibly be overcome," Julie said. Hannah looked up at her sharply and shook her head. Julie pointedly didn't look directly at her. "First, we need the name of the lawyer."

"Joseph didn't tell me."

"But he probably would," Julie said, "if you asked him."

Hannah gave her another sharp shake of her head and again Julie ignored her.

Daniel set down the apple and wiped his hands on the edge of his apron. He fished out his cellphone from his hip pocket. The call was quick and efficient. "Joseph said the lawyer's name was Randall Cantor."

Julie looked up the attorney in the phone book stuffed into a row of cookbooks on the kitchen's narrow bookshelf. She knew the address, though she'd never noticed a law office on that street. It was downtown. "Everything's quiet here. I think I'll drive over and meet Mr. Cantor. You care to come?"

Again Hannah shook her head, adding a fierce glare this time, but Julie kept most of her attention firmly on Daniel. He turned to Hannah. "I hate to bail in the middle of the tarts."

"That's fine." Hannah's response sounded slightly less gracious through clenched teeth. "I can finish."

Julie held up a hand. "On second thought, stay here for a bit longer. I want to ask Shirley about Cantor. I've yet to hear of anyone in Straussberg that Shirley doesn't know something about."

"Fine with me." Daniel walked over to wash his hands. "That woman scares me. I think it's the hair."

As Julie expected, Shirley had lots of opinions about the lawyer, and not one of them was good. "That one has a reputation sure enough—a reputation for doing anything for his client for enough money. He's about as ethical as a shark."

But is he as deadly? Julie wondered.

She collected Daniel, and they drove into downtown Straussberg. The sun was warm, but the breeze was chilly, making scarlet and gold leaves skip and scuttle along the sidewalks. They parked in the complimentary visitor's lot and made the hike to the office. Though small, the office was neat and the furniture looked new. Julie didn't care for the style, all metal and sharp angles, but it did hint of more success than the cramped space implied.

When Julie asked to see Mr. Cantor, the woman turned

up her sharply pointed nose and asked, "Do you have an appointment?"

"No, but you can tell him it's in reference to the sale of the Winkler farm."

The receptionist narrowed her eyes but passed along the message. In moments, a door opened and a thick man with the face of a dyspeptic bulldog walked out. "Mr. and Mrs. Winkler? Please, come in."

Julie ignored the implied question. She reached out and squeezed Daniel's hand, giving him a warning glance. "Thank you. You were interested in buying the farm?"

Cantor led them into his office, which matched the reception room in size and style. "I'm empowered to operate on behalf of an interested party."

"We'd like to know his name."

The lawyer's smile tightened. "That I can't tell you, Mrs. Winkler. The buyer insists upon staying anonymous." He turned his attention from her to Daniel. "But I can assure you, Mr. Winkler, this is a legitimate offer. The buyer has the means to pay."

"I'm surprised the offer is still on the table," Julie said, "what with all the excavating that's already been done."

The lawyer glanced back at her, clearly annoyed that she kept talking. "It's nothing that can't be repaired." Again he turned to Daniel. "My client has authorized me to offer another twenty thousand above the previous offer, Mr. Winkler, but the excavation must not start back up."

Before Julie could comment, Daniel shook his head at her. "I'm not Mr. Winkler. I'm Mr. Franklin."

The lawyer stiffened. "It's not wise to come in here pretending to be the Winklers."

"We didn't pretend," Julie said. "You assumed. We're

not legally responsible for your assumptions."

Cantor narrowed his eyes at her. "And you're Mr. Franklin's lawyer?"

She smiled sweetly. "I'm not legally obligated to identify myself either, but the police are likely to be interested in your client. After all, he wanted the excavation shut down very badly. Killing George Benning was an extreme but efficient way to accomplish the shutdown."

The lawyer glared at her for a moment, then turned to Daniel. "I would think you wouldn't be interested in provoking more trouble, Mr. Franklin."

"What's that supposed to mean?" Daniel demanded.

"You are now the prime suspect in a murder, are you not?" the lawyer asked.

Julie cut in before Daniel could answer. "He won't be when the police hear about your client and the extreme lengths he's gone to in order to purchase the farm. The fact that you've made the effort to be informed about the murder tells me you're well aware of the peril your client is in."

The lawyer smiled. "Or maybe I'm just nosy." At that, a curl of classical music slipped from the lawyer's pocket. He pulled out his cellphone, glanced at the screen, and said to Julie, "This meeting is over. I'm sure you can let yourselves out." He herded them toward the door and then shut it as soon as they'd passed the threshold.

"That wasn't exactly productive," Daniel said, his expression dark.

Julie smiled. "The day is young. Come on."

With a little coaxing, Julie soon had Daniel set up in the coffee shop across the street from the lawyer's door. He'd watch the building and call Julie as soon as both the lawyer and his receptionist left for the day. "I'll come back, and we'll find out what the lawyer knows," she said.

"I'm not certain I want to be involved in breaking and entering," Daniel whispered fiercely, his gaze darting around the coffee shop.

"It's better than being suspected in a murder."

"What if this shop closes before the lawyer's office? Am I supposed to try loitering? I'm not the most inconspicuous guy."

"This shop is open late. I checked. You'll be fine."

To be honest, Daniel didn't look like he'd be fine. He looked a little like he'd be sick, but Julie believed in thinking positively. She went back to being an innkeeper as she waited for Daniel's call.

Evening had settled a blanket of gray over the town before Daniel finally called, his voice only slightly panicky. Julie returned to the coffee shop as quickly as speed limits allowed. She found Daniel pacing while the young barista watched him curiously. "You weren't kidding about the 'not being inconspicuous' thing."

"Sorry," he muttered. "This is a little outside my skill set. What I'd like to know is why it's not outside yours."

"I've lived an interesting life. Now, it's time for a little romantic stroll."

"Romantic?" His eyes took on a new gleam.

Julie coughed nervously. "Think of it as camouflage. Just put your arm around me, and let's go."

As they left the shop and strolled across the street, Julie turned frequently to murmur encouraging things to Daniel. At first his arm around her felt stiff, but he eventually began to settle into his role as they stood on the sidewalk. Julie gave the lock on the lawyer's door sideward glances.

"Now, time to back me up against the door," she said, and Daniel followed her directions—a little too well.

"Whoa!" she said as his face closed in on hers. "Wh-what are you doing?"

He stopped, his lips mere inches from her own. "I thought you wanted me to kiss you."

She let out a nervous snort and immediately wished she could take it back. *Get a grip, Julie.* Clearing her throat, she ignored his captivating blue-gray eyes and said, "I want you to stay focused on the task at hand. How could I possibly see anything with your face smushed against mine?"

With a slight frown, he pulled his head back. "Better?"

No. "Just lean your body in close. You're a lot bigger than me, so you'll help hide what I'm doing." She squirmed around in the tight confines so she could reach the lock. She pulled her lock picks out of her blazer pocket and quickly opened the door.

They slipped inside. Daniel reached for the light switch, but Julie caught his hand. "No lights. We're trying for low profile."

"Right. If I trip over something and break a leg, will that be low enough?"

Julie fired up the flashlight app on her phone and quickly crossed the room, only to discover the door to the lawyer's office was locked as well. She picked it quickly. The lawyer had chosen cheap over secure.

"Now that we're illegally inside, what do we do?" Daniel asked.

"We search."

"For what?"

"Clues. Didn't you ever read the Hardy Boys when you were a kid?"

He shook his head. "I favored nonfiction."

Julie picked the locks on several file cabinets, but none

of the files jumped out at her as the possible mystery client. She stood up and stretched, turning around to consider other places to search. Daniel stood in front of a large aquarium, peering in. "I don't think you'll find any clues in there."

"I'm not likely to find any here at all," he said. "I'm just along for the terror. The fish make me feel calmer."

Julie glanced in the tank but then wrinkled her nose at the fishy scent of the water. She decided instead to search the lawyer's desk, starting with his datebook. She flipped through, paying special attention to the day of the offer on the farm. She'd begun to lose hope when she noticed a pattern of conference calls with someone designated as "SEN." She tugged on Daniel's jacket. "Look at this."

He turned to look. "'SEN about GA,'" he read aloud. "Is that supposed to mean something? Maybe he's considering a trip to Georgia."

"If so, it requires a lot of conference calls. What if 'GA' is *'Grand Adventure'*?"

Daniel looked again at the datebook. "Then who's 'SEN'?"

"That's the million-dollar question," she said. "I'm going back through the files to see if I can find anyone with the initials S-E-N."

"Or anyone whose name begins with 'SEN,'" Daniel suggested.

"Good idea." Julie turned back to the file cabinet and froze. A large window stretched over much of the wall above the file cabinets. Though it was covered with thick blinds, she could make out flashing lights around them. She peeked through the slats. Two police cars sat on the street in front of the office and another was pulling up. "Time to go."

"Why?"

"Police."

"Swell. Glad I asked." Daniel headed for the door that led to the receptionist's office, and Julie followed. She passed him and cracked open the door to the hall beyond. She could see the police massing outside, flashlights sweeping across the thin, frosted windows on either side of the outer door.

"We can't get out that way," she whispered. She turned to look in the opposite direction. Narrow stairs led up to a second floor, but Julie would rather not be trapped above the lawyer's office if she could avoid it. So she dragged Daniel out of the office and towed him away from the street-side door. The hall was narrow because of the stairs and they had to move in single file.

Julie opened the next door in the hall. It led to an outdated bathroom. A quick glace showed no window big enough to get out. She closed the door and hurried to the end of the short hall. From the lawyer's office it had looked like a dead end, but once they reached it, they saw the stairs had hidden another door. Julie quickly turned the lock and they rushed outside.

The door led to a tiny garden space. Three other buildings had back doors leading into the courtyard space, but there was no obvious way to get out of it. Julie pointed across to the building on the other side. A rickety metal fire escape was bolted into the brick. "This time we climb."

They scrambled up the fire escape as quickly as they dared. The metal creaked and groaned, making stealth impossible. Finally they hit the last landing and found a metal ladder bolted to the wall that led to the roof of the building. "I hope you're not afraid of heights."

"Not at all," he said. "Ladies first."

As soon as they'd both scrambled onto the roof of the building, the back door to the lawyer's office burst open and several policemen hurried outside. Julie and Daniel ducked down, barely peeking over the edge. "Watch them," she whispered.

She quickly searched the roof of the building for signs of a door leading inside or even another fire escape that would take them to an empty street. She found neither. If the police climbed the ladder, they'd be caught.

ELEVEN

On the flat roof of the building, Julie squatted at Daniel's side, her heart pounding as she watched the police. Her leg muscles complained about the combination of her awkward squat and her tension. After what seemed like an eternity, the officers finished their search of the small courtyard garden and walked back into the lawyer's office. They didn't come out again. Julie moved to peer off a different side of the building. After a long, chilly wait, the police cars drove past on the street below her.

Once back down in the garden, Julie picked the lock on another building, and they found themselves in the storage room of a thrift shop. They left through the front door. Julie used her lock picks to lock up after them, and they drove in exhausted silence to the inn.

After Daniel went upstairs, Julie found Hannah in the kitchen with a large bowl hugged close to her chest as she beat eggs fiercely with a wire whisk. "Don't you have a mixer for that?"

"Sometimes I like the hands-on approach."

Julie fished in the basket on the counter for a decaf coffee pod. She dropped it in the coffee maker and snapped the top down. Then she watched her friend abuse the eggs for a while.

"You disappeared right after supper," Hannah said.

"I went to check out the lawyer's office, the one who made the offer on the Winkler farm."

Hannah sighed and beat harder. "I don't suppose the lawyer was there."

"It's easier when they aren't."

"I'm glad you weren't arrested."

"It was a close call, but we managed." Julie turned to collect her filled cup of coffee.

"That's fortunate, because coming to bail you out would have been a problem. I have to get this custard made and then dough for the tart shells if we're going to have quiche for breakfast."

"I wouldn't have wanted to inconvenience you."

Hannah stopped whipping and shoved the bowl away. "So what can I do?"

"Do?"

"You're neck deep in something you should have stayed far away from, and you want me to do something to help. I can tell. Cough it up. What do you want?"

"You're getting very grumpy."

"I've always been grumpy. Now out with it."

Julie quickly told her about the lawyer's datebook and the conference calls. "I need you to gather all the information you can about Randall Cantor, and see if you can find ties to anyone with the initials S-E-N or maybe someone whose name begins with 'SEN.'"

Hannah gave her a long, flat stare, then walked to the kitchen to pull out a hunk of Swiss cheese and a carton of cream. She set them on the counter with slightly more force than necessary. Then she retrieved a cheese grater from one of the cupboards and raked the cheese over it.

"Are you waiting for a magic word?" Julie asked. "Please?"

"If I refuse, I suppose you'll find some more dangerous way to get the information."

"There is that possibility."

"Why didn't we just stay in New York and let the art ring find us there?" Hannah asked. "Why come here and pretend we're going to do something different?" She pointed the tattered hunk of Swiss at Julie. "I *like* it here." Then she plopped the cheese back on the grater and raked shreds off into the growing pile.

"So do I, but I can't just ignore this. I liked George and now he's dead. I have to help find his killer."

"Julie, that's why we have police. They're trained in criminal investigation, and they get paid for it." Again Hannah pointed the cheese. "You barely even knew George. You want to get involved because it's *exciting*, and you miss that. You might as well be honest."

"Yes, I do miss the excitement, but I also want to help find George's killer. One desire doesn't negate the other."

Hannah slammed the cheese down on the counter. "Unfortunately, the one sure way I know to find out who this 'SEN' person might be is a search of Cantor's phone records. Matching up the conference calls would be easy enough."

"Then do that."

"I can't hack into the phone company without breaking at least as many laws as you just did, and *I'm* not in the business of law breaking anymore. *I'm* a cook. Cooks don't do things like that."

"You've done it before."

"I don't want to go back to breaking the law on a regular basis. I'm happier now. I like cooking. It's orderly and precise and it makes people happy. It also doesn't draw the attention of the wrong sort of people, which is what you seem intent on doing."

"So you won't help?"

"I'll feed you some really nice quiche in the morning, but I won't break the law—again."

Julie sipped her coffee in silence as her mind raced through her options. Julie's skill set had never really extended to techy bits and bytes. She was great at breaking into real places, but not so much with virtual ones.

She sighed. The phone records would have made it so easy. Then her eyes widened. "The phone!"

Hannah glanced up. "What phone?"

"The lawyer's phone. It should have his contacts on it. I saw him use it at work, so there's every chance the mysterious SEN is in his contacts." Julie drummed her fingers against her mug.

Hannah scooped up a handful of cheese and dumped it in her egg bowl, then added cream and stirred them in. "You're going to steal his phone, aren't you?"

"Pretty much, yeah."

Julie left Hannah brutalizing more breakfast prep and settled into her sitting room with a pad and pencil to plan her phone acquisition. She knew Hannah considered her too impulsive, but the truth was, she actually preferred a good plan. She was simply always prepared to improvise when necessary.

A knock on the door drew her attention away from the list. "Julie?"

"Come in, Daniel."

For a moment, the door remained closed. Julie wondered if Daniel was readying himself for some kind of confrontation. When he did walk in, she noted that the lines around his eyes looked sharper and his damp hair stood up wildly.

He settled into the seat across from her. "How can you look so unruffled after this evening?"

Julie waved a dismissive hand. "We need to find out who the mysterious SEN is."

"We almost got arrested."

"But we didn't." She twisted her hair into a messy bun and stuck the pencil through it to keep it up. Then she set her list aside. "And we learned something important."

"That I'm not cut out for a life of crime?"

Julie grinned. "I already figured that. No, we have a lead on the person who has a *real* motive in the murder. We find that person, figure out the motive, hand it over to the police detective, and his interest in you will dry up. Then you'll be able to get back to work on the farm."

"You make it sound so simple."

"Simple it is. Easy? Not so much. I'll know more after I get Cantor's phone tomorrow."

Daniel shook his head. "Do I want to know how you're going to do that?"

She set her chair rocking with a push of her toes. "Probably. But I'll tell you after the fact. It'll be easier on your nerves. Now, are you sure the initials S-E-N don't mean anything to you? Realistically, if someone is trying to shut down the dig, it would be someone who is somehow related to the ship."

"The ship sank in 1856," he said. "I don't know why anyone would be interested in it today."

"Maybe it's someone who wants the fame of digging it up himself. Do you have competitors?"

"I know of a few historians who have shown a mild interest in my research, but nothing serious. I don't know of anyone I'd actually call a competitor."

"Well, when I have the phone, we can see if you recognize any of his contacts. If you do, that will be a big clue right there."

Daniel leaned back in the chair and closed his eyes. He looked tired, almost ill.

"I'm really sorry about George," she said softly.

"I talked to his mom after we got back. They're sending the body to her in Tennessee as soon as the coroner releases it. He has a sister there too, so his mom isn't alone." He opened his eyes and looked at Julie. "They'll let me know when the funeral is set. I'll go, of course."

"Of course."

He shook his head slowly. "This was going to be a big adventure for both of us. George was humoring me, but he was having fun too. We didn't get to spend time together all that often."

Julie didn't know what to say. Daniel sat back again with his eyes closed. Her life had been filled with casual connections, mostly because she preferred it that way. Her parents died when she was barely eighteen. She knew none of her extended family. She'd only grown close to two people in her adult life: Hannah, who was like a sister to her, and her boss and mentor, Jonathan Hunt.

At some point, Jonathan had turned from mentor to suitor, so Julie left—left him and left the company. She started her own antiquities recovery business in New York City. A few months after she'd opened, Hannah had shown up on her doorstep, explaining that working for Jonathan was too dull without her.

Julie looked at Daniel in the soft lighting. She imagined Hannah getting hurt because of her. One thing was for sure. If it happened, she would find out who hurt her friend, and she'd make him pay.

Daniel opened his eyes again. "You're looking fierce."

"Just thinking. Look, you're practically asleep in that chair. You should go to bed."

He heaved himself to his feet and pointed at Julie's pad of paper. "Be careful, please. I don't want any more friends hurt because of my treasure hunting."

She was startled by how much his words mirrored what she'd just been thinking. "I'll be careful. Sleep well."

After lunch the next day, Julie took a walk. It felt good to stretch her long legs, and she remembered seeing a phone store only a few blocks away. When she got there, she bought the exact same cellphone Cantor had pulled from his pocket. She carried the phone around behind the building and used a piece of brick to bust the phone to pieces. She carefully picked up all the tiny bits and slipped them into the pocket of her brushed corduroy blazer.

When she got back to the inn, she found Shirley and Inga standing with their backs to her, chatting at the front desk. Julie was so surprised by the unlikely pair that she paused just inside the front door and watched them for a moment.

The housekeeper stood as stiffly as a guard at Buckingham Palace and nearly as grim. "You should consider the reputation of this inn," she said.

"Reputation is lovely, Inga," Shirley insisted. "But money is more important. The guests love my Stitches and Stories. And they're fun."

Inga sniffed. "They're silly. You should make the stories more about stitches and less about made-up stories."

It was Shirley's turn to look offended. "I research my stories very carefully."

"Really?" Inga scoffed. "Bigfoot?"

Shirley's offense dissolved into giggles. "You sound like Julie."

"I doubt that." Inga's tone was so disapproving that Julie couldn't help but feel a little offended.

She cleared her throat and walked up to the front desk. "Good afternoon."

"Did you have a nice walk?" Shirley asked brightly.

"I did."

Inga turned her expressionless face toward Julie. "Excuse me, please. I need to take a walk of my own around the yard. Yesterday I found a foam coffee cup crammed in the fencing."

"I very much appreciate your hard work."

Inga looked dubious. "You'll need to contact the gardener. The last rain brought down sticks in the yard. I don't collect sticks."

"I'll do that."

Inga spun on her heel and walked away. Before she reached the front door, Shirley called after her. "Will I see you Friday night?"

Inga turned, her face nearly frozen with shock. "We shall see." Then she practically ran out of the house.

"What are you two doing this weekend?" Julie asked.

Shirley leaned in close and whispered loudly, "It's a secret, but let's just say that there are hidden depths to Inga you would never suspect."

"I don't doubt it."

Shirley bustled off to the tearoom while Julie pondered the hidden depths for a moment. The rest of the afternoon passed in relative calm, and Julie didn't feel too guilty for slipping away to stake out the lawyer's office.

She loitered on the street for barely half an hour, peering in windows and keeping a casual eye on the office, before the lawyer emerged from his office. He was talking on his cellphone as he headed for the curb where a row of cars were parked.

Julie sprinted toward him. "Mr. Cantor!"

He held the phone away from his ear slightly as he turned and watched her rapid approach. His frown of annoyance quickly turned to alarm when Julie didn't slow down. He took a step back away from her, then another one.

Since he was already close to the curb, his backing away quickly brought him to the edge, and he stumbled. He pinwheeled his arms, trying to catch his balance. Julie lunged forward for the last couple feet between them. She reached out as if to grab his arm and keep him from falling. Instead, she knocked his arm hard, sending him into the street.

He landed on the ground with a thud, and his phone flew out of his hand, slamming into the pavement. Julie rushed after it as she dipped her hand into the pocket of her jacket. She tossed the bits into the street as she reached for the phone. She scooped up the phone, pocketed it, and stomped down on one of the larger pieces of phone all in one smooth move. "Oh, no! I'm so sorry."

"What do you think you're doing, you ... you ... *crazy* woman!" he sputtered.

"I'm so sorry. I was only trying to help." She held out a hand, but he ignored it as he scrambled to his feet.

"*Help*? You knocked me down!"

She blinked at him, her eyes wide. "You fell! I was trying to catch you!"

"I don't know what you're up to, but I have half a mind to call the police and have you charged with assault."

"I didn't assault you," she insisted, adding a tremble to her voice. "I tried to keep you from falling. Look, send a bill for the phone to the Quilt Haus Inn. I'll be happy to pay for it since you seem to think it was my fault, but I *didn't* knock you down."

His voice rose to a shriek as he called her a very rude name. Julie gave a little hiccup and looked as hurt as she could manage.

"Hey, leave that poor girl alone!"

Julie turned to look for her new ally. An older man in a long trench coat waved his cane at the lawyer. "I saw everything. You tripped over your own big fat feet."

Cantor pointed an angry finger at the spectator. "You stay out of this, old man!"

At that, more catcalls came from the small crowd beginning to form on the sidewalk. Clearly no one was going to side with the lawyer over Julie.

Seeing he was outnumbered, Cantor snarled and stomped over to his car. He hauled open the driver's-side door, then turned to glare at Julie. "You'll be hearing from me."

The crowd shouted him down, and the lawyer gave up and drove away. Julie stood still, gazing after his car and slowly shaking her head. A tall elderly woman whose pewter curls contrasted sharply with her warm brown skin stepped off the curb and marched up to Julie. She put an arm around her and said, "It's all right, dear. Pull yourself together and hold your head high. People like that just like picking on the small folks."

Julie nodded and sniffled. "I don't know why he said those dreadful things."

"He was embarrassed, I expect. Men can be such babies." The woman herded her onto the sidewalk, then insisted on walking with Julie to her car. "You go on home and get a nice cup of tea."

"I will. Thank you."

Once back at the inn, Julie patiently sat through Hannah's scolding, waiting for her to run out of steam.

"You worry too much," she said as soon as her friend wound down. "Cantor didn't even come close to figuring out what happened."

"You're right." Hannah peered at the face of the phone. "I should be more worried about how good you are at this kind of behavior."

The door to the kitchen swung open, and Shirley poked her head in. "Someone's at the front desk for you, Julie."

"I'm coming." Julie turned to Hannah. "Get what you can from this?"

Hannah nodded without looking up, so Julie followed Shirley out to the front desk. A middle-aged woman in the typical tourist uniform of comfortable slacks and good walking shoes stood clutching a big shopping bag from the quirky home decor store across the road. Her face brightened when she saw Julie approach.

"I was shopping across the street, and the owner told me about this inn." The woman's voice was soft and tentative, going up at the end of each sentence as if questioning her own statements. "You hold quilt retreats here?"

"We do, but we only have a handful of big scheduled retreat events each year," Julie said.

"But a quilting group could have their own mini retreat here anytime? I am part of a quilt club in Kentucky. I think they'd love it here."

"We would be happy to host a retreat for your group. We do mini-retreats all the time," Julie said. "How many quilters are in your group?"

The woman continued to offer hesitant answers to Julie's questions, though her volume did increase slightly as she grew more excited about the idea. Julie took the woman on a tour of the inn and enjoyed seeing her face light up with each new room.

"I can't actually book anything now," the woman said. "But I'll tell my group as soon as I get home. I know they'll love the idea!"

"I hope so," Julie said. "Do remember that for a large group, we'll need to book at least a month ahead."

"I'll remember."

Then Shirley scooped the quiet woman up and swept her off to the tearoom. Julie hoped she still wanted to have a quilt retreat at the inn after a visit with Shirley. She looked toward the breakfast room, wondering if she dared dash in to see what Hannah might have learned from the phone. Then she shook her head; better to wait until suppertime.

She picked through the stack of mail she still hadn't opened. The bills she slipped into the box for dealing with right away. The circulars for various deals she dropped into the trash behind the desk. Then she frowned at the last item. It was a small envelope with her name and the inn's address hand-printed in precise block letters. It bore no return address.

Inside she found a collection of torn bits of paper. She shook them out onto the desk and pieced them back together. It was a photo of her at the front desk. Someone had drawn a red X over her face, then had torn up the photo and shoved it into the envelope. There was no actual written threat attached, but she felt decidedly unsettled. This message was definitely for her, and it wasn't friendly.

She decided not to share it with either Hannah or Daniel. They were both worked up enough already. She considered dropping the torn pieces in the trash but decided instead to slip them back into the envelope. She might want them later.

To take her mind off the note, Julie threw herself into bill paying and managed to lose track of time as she wrestled with the numbers. When she did make it back to the kitchen, the cozy smell of soup wrapped around her. "That smells fantastic."

"Vegetable barley soup," Hannah said. "I'm testing some soup recipes. I wonder if we might consider adding soup and sandwiches to the tearoom menu at lunchtime."

"Lovely idea. Are you going to tell me what you found on the phone or just torture me with soup?"

Hannah turned to stir the pot of soup, then heaved it onto a large trivet on the counter, where she added some browned, crumbled sausage. Julie looked at the huge pot with a frown. "Isn't that a lot of soup for the two of us?"

"I'm freezing the leftovers." Hannah wiped her hands on a dish towel. "I didn't find any mysterious text messages related to the dig at Winkler Farm. So whatever communication he's had by phone has either been verbal, or he's been careful to delete it."

"Not surprising. Lawyers are paranoid creatures," Julie said.

Hannah raised an eyebrow. "Not like you've given this guy any reason to be paranoid. At any rate, I went through his contacts list. I found five possible connections to S-E-N." She fished in the pocket of her apron, pulled out an index card, and handed it to Julie.

"Fantastic!" Julie looked over the list as Hannah pointed at each item.

"This one is probably a stretch," Hannah said. "Maxwell Cantor Sr. I checked online. He's the lawyer's uncle. I know 'senior' is normally abbreviated as 'S-R,' but I thought maybe the lawyer was using an unusual form to make it harder to guess who he was referencing."

Julie wrinkled her nose. "That does seem like a stretch."

Hannah pointed farther down the list. "These two are Missouri state senators: Walter Parson and Lucas North. And this one, Steven E. Needlemeyer, he might be identified by the initials S-E-N. I only found one woman: Lila Huff Seneca."

Julie tapped the paper. "That's interesting. I met Walter Parson's wife recently. She came to talk about having a fundraiser at the inn. Now his name turns up on the list."

"Life does have coincidences."

"But they're always worth noticing."

Hannah shrugged. "Did she seem weird?"

"No. Actually she was very nice. Inga even liked her."

"Now that *is* weird." Hannah turned back to the pot and dipped out a crock of soup. She set it in front of Julie. "Eat. Tell me what you think."

Julie continued to study the list as she took a sip of the soup. She felt certain someone on the list had something to do with George's death. Now the only question was, which one of the names was the mysterious "SEN"?

TWELVE

W hen she finally headed upstairs for the night, she tapped on Daniel's door. As soon as the door cracked, she held up the list. "We have suspects."

He looked at the list suspiciously, then opened the door. "Are we going to break into their homes?"

"For the record, breaking and entering isn't usually my first contact choice." The tower room didn't have a separate sitting room, only a small alcove with a love seat and chair. Julie felt a bit awkward with the bed in view after their recent close encounter, but she perched on the arm of the small love seat. Daniel sank into the other end of the love seat and read the list. She gave him a moment, then asked, "Do any of the names sound familiar from your research?"

He shook his head. "None of the last names match the captain or anyone on the crew list of *The Grand Adventure*."

Julie thought about mentioning Senator Parson's wife but decided not to muddy the waters. She'd keep it in mind when they talked to the senator, but it would be good for one of them to be completely impartial. And she honestly couldn't picture the pleasant woman she'd met attacking a grown man like George.

He looked up from the list. "So, what's the plan? Do we stake out each of them?"

"I thought we might talk to them and see what happens. After all, just the sight of you might provoke a reaction."

"If the reaction is to try to kill me, I'm not a fan of this idea."

"I suspect we won't be attacked on anyone's doorstep." Julie looked around the room and spotted Daniel's laptop at the small writing desk tucked next to the bed. "We can probably look them up online and get addresses."

Though the Wi-Fi on the third floor was a little slow, they managed to find each of the people on the list. Lila Huff Seneca proved to be the toughest, until they realized that her last name wasn't "Seneca." Her name was Lila Huff, and she was a member of the Seneca nation of Native Americans.

Daniel tapped the paper. "We should start with Lila Huff."

"Because she took the longest to find?"

"Because she's the only woman on the list."

Julie frowned. "And?"

He shrugged. "I could probably take her in a fight."

That made Julie laugh. "Great. I'll get Hannah to cover for me after we finish breakfast tomorrow, and we'll see what we can learn about Ms. Huff."

The next morning, Julie accepted a ride in Daniel's truck and enjoyed the chance to sightsee a little. They passed acres of cultivated land that rolled and dipped gently like a brown-and-gold sea. Clouds hung low in the sky, their bellies a pale gray. They passed a pond whose waters were so still they reflected the clouds and trees like glass.

Some of the places Julie had visited in her antiquities recovery work would sound exotic to the inhabitants of the homes they drove past—places like Paris and Rome and Beijing. But to Julie, the rolling countryside and its peacefulness were a better kind of exotic and enticing. She was definitely coming to appreciate her new home—aside from the murder and the cryptic threats.

When they reached Washington's downtown, Julie was struck by how similar the river town looked to Straussberg, with the same tall, narrow brick buildings and mix of architectural styles including stately Victorians, Greek Revival, and Georgian. They passed through the downtown and continued into the residential area, finally pulling up in front of an older home with a rock-clad first floor and clapboard second story. Above a small door leading into the first floor hung a sign that read "Basket Shop."

"She lives over her shop," Julie observed.

"So it seems. How are we going to explain showing up at her door?"

"Just follow my lead. The fact that her door is public will make this much easier than I'd anticipated."

Julie hopped out of the truck and headed into the shop. The interior walls were rock like the outside, and the place had a warm, dark-honey–colored wood floor. Rough shelves covered the walls, and freestanding display racks dotted the room. Every surface was covered with baskets in different styles and shapes and materials.

Julie caught the eye of the attractive woman behind the counter and asked, "Do you make all these?"

The woman laughed. "You give me far more credit than I deserve." Her smile warmed her dark eyes as she gestured around the room. "These baskets come from all over the United States. I make a few, but I also get pieces from other artisans."

"But they're all handmade?"

The woman nodded.

Julie drifted closer to the counter. She saw a pile of business cards and picked one up. "You're Lila Huff?"

"I am."

"What got you started in this craft?"

"Basket making is a reflection of the history and culture of the person making it, as well as the ingenuity of the basket maker's use of materials. I have many baskets that reflect a wealth of Native American traditions."

Daniel walked up beside Julie carrying a small round basket. He held it up. "This is impressive. I've always enjoyed the use of pine needles in coiled baskets. Did you make it?"

"No. I work in traditional Seneca ash splint basketry."

"Can you show me one?" Julie asked.

The basket Lila showed her was tightly woven from narrow ash splints. Julie decided to buy one for Hannah. As she paid, she said, "Washington is a charming town. I've recently moved to Straussberg; have you ever been there?"

Lila shook her head. "I'm afraid I'm a recent transplant myself. I'm originally from upstate New York, but my husband loves this area."

"There's certainly a lot of rich history here," Julie said as she watched the other woman closely. "Daniel here is a historian. He's excavating an old steamboat that was sunk on the Missouri River."

Lila's eyes lit up. "That must be fascinating work. Is it hard to dive on a wreck in the river? I would think the current must be an issue."

Julie forced a laugh and said, "That's the amazing part. It's not in the river. The course of the river shifted many moons ago, and the wreck is in someone's farm field." Julie would have sworn Lila's look of surprise was genuine.

"When I begin bringing up artifacts," Daniel said, "I'm going to be in need of experts in different handcrafts and arts. It looks like you might be someone to ask about baskets."

"I have made a study of native basketry, but I'm sure you could find someone who knows a lot more, though I'd love to look at any baskets you find." Lila pointed at her business card in Julie's hand. "Feel free to call if you think I could help. I could probably place a basket in the general region it was made and tell you about materials, though you might know as much as me, considering how well you spotted the pine needle coil basket."

Daniel tapped the desk. "You know, I think your name sounds familiar. A lawyer friend of mine may have mentioned you—Randall Cantor?"

Lila looked skeptical. "I didn't think I made that much of an impression on Mr. Cantor. He's looking into some copyright matters for me. I'm working on a book about Native American basketry. It's becoming a lost art. But I honestly don't think your lawyer friend is very interested in art."

After a few more minutes of friendly conversation, Daniel and Julie took their leave. Daniel turned to Julie as they crossed the small parking lot. "She didn't exactly strike me as the murdering type," he said.

"I'm not sure there is a type, but she certainly didn't act like she recognized you or anything related to the ship. I think we can safely mark her off the list."

Daniel hauled the truck door open for her. "Great. Can we get some lunch now? I'm starving."

"Sure. Then we'll check in on Steven E. Needlemeyer." Julie hopped up onto the seat.

"Doesn't he live over in Chamois?" Daniel asked. "Do you want to be away from the inn so long?"

Julie snapped her seat belt. "Needlemeyer lives in Chamois, but he works in Straussberg."

"That would be convenient for murder. Why didn't we check him first?"

Julie shrugged. "You wanted to go to Washington."

They stopped for lunch at a local winery. The flower beds, arched brick doorway, and heavy antique door of the restaurant gave the impression of stepping back in time as they walked in.

Julie blinked as she adjusted to the light inside the restaurant. The ceiling was crossed with heavy timbers of dark, weathered wood. The tables were heavy and plain. Though not rough, they had a similar weathered look. Beautiful woven cloth place mats marked each place setting.

The menu leaned heavily toward German dishes and suggested different wines to go with each selection. The rich smells of meat and spice made Julie's stomach growl as she read through the selections. She liked German food, but she hadn't had much experience with it outside of Hannah's cooking, so some of the items on the menu looked a bit mysterious. She finally settled on the *Krautrouladen*, as she generally liked cabbage rolls. Daniel ordered *Jägerschnitzel*, pork cutlets in gravy.

Julie handed her menu back to the waiter and sipped her water. Her stomach growled loudly. "Quick, take my mind off food before someone calls animal control."

"OK. Tell me, how does a woman who has a penchant for breaking and entering end up in Straussberg, Missouri, managing a quilter's inn?" Daniel asked.

"I was looking for a change of scenery from New York City."

"Where you were a cat burglar?"

She shook her head and looked around the room as if fascinated by the woodwork. "I was in antiques."

"At an antique shop?" The crease between his eyebrows deepened. "You did a lot of lock picking there?"

She smiled, seizing on a possible answer that wasn't exactly a lie. "You'd be amazed at how many locked drawers and locked trunks are out there—pieces where the key hasn't been matched to the lock in decades." She knew that was true. The head of an antiques auction house had told her so while she picked the lock on an antique desk she'd acquired for him. The lock had been surprisingly stubborn, and it made Julie glad that most of the locks she picked were much newer.

"I just can't picture you toiling away in an antiques shop," he said.

She smiled in return. "You've seen me toiling away in an inn. It's really not that much different."

He studied her in silence. She fought the urge to squirm beneath his piercing gaze and kept a pleasant smile.

Finally he said, "Considering I'm going along with you on this crime spree to find George's killer, I wish you'd be honest with me."

"We're not on a crime spree." She went for the water glass again, but Daniel reached out and laid a hand on hers.

He continued to look at her intently. "Why don't you trust me?"

"I do." Julie eased her hand out from under his and brought the glass of water to her lips.

He gave up then, and the rest of the lunch was quiet. The food tasted excellent, tender and bursting with flavor, but somehow it seemed difficult to swallow with the cloud of Daniel's disappointment hanging over them. She was glad when they were back on the road.

Needlemeyer Construction had an office at the edge

of Straussberg's commercial district, nearly as far from the Quilt Haus Inn as possible without heading into vineyards and farmland. Daniel pulled into the parking lot of the small strip of interconnected businesses. The construction company was nestled between a bank and an optometrist.

They walked into the reception area, where a man was bent over the receptionist's desk, pointing to her computer screen while she nodded and typed. They both looked up as Daniel and Julie entered.

"Steven Needlemeyer?" Daniel asked.

The man stood, taking off the glasses perched on his nose. He slipped them into his pocket and held out a calloused hand. "The same."

They shook, and Daniel introduced himself and Julie. "If you have a minute, I'm in the early stages of shopping for a construction company to build a steamboat museum."

"Sounds like an interesting project." Needlemeyer looked at his watch. "I have an appointment pretty soon, but I can spare a few minutes now if you want to talk about it."

As the builder ushered them into his office, Daniel continued to talk. "I actually have a site for the museum. It's an old factory building, so I suppose I'm looking at more of a remodel than new construction."

"That can be even more challenging."

"True, but visitors love to see historical museums in historical buildings."

They chatted about the project for several minutes, and Julie was amazed at how passionately Daniel spoke. It was clear he really did intend to build the museum once *The Grand Adventure* was recovered. It was also clear that

Steven Needlemeyer had exactly zero interest in the actual excavation of the steamboat. Each time Daniel brought it up, he responded politely but steered the conversation back around to the remodel.

As soon as Julie ruled the builder out as the murderer, she lost interest in the conversation. To avoid distracting the men by fidgeting, she excused herself, citing a need for the powder room.

As she breezed out of the office, she thought about the euphemism "powder room." She'd never powdered anything in a ladies' restroom in her life. When she reached the receptionist's desk, the young woman chirped a happy "Can I help you?"

"No, actually I got bored," Julie admitted. "I can only offer so much moral support, you know what I mean?"

The woman nodded so enthusiastically that her wire-frame glasses slid down her nose. "Uncle Steven is a sweetie, but all this construction stuff can be a snooze."

Although she'd really already written off the builder as a guilty party, Julie still couldn't resist fishing a little. "The only thing more boring about this process was the trip to Randall Cantor's office to sign a mountain of papers."

"Oh!" The receptionist dropped her voice to a bare whisper. "Don't mention Cantor in front of Uncle Steven. They don't get along *at all*."

"Really? No surprise, I guess. I kind of thought the lawyer was a jerk," Julie said in a matching whisper.

The receptionist sniffed in disdain. "He's a pig. Unfortunately, Steven is dating the lawyer's mom, so he has a tough time avoiding the jerk."

"That must be hard."

"Don't get me wrong," the young woman insisted.

"Elizabeth is a sweetie, just like Uncle Steven. But her son …" She gave a dainty shudder. "It's obvious why the guy's not married. Who could put up with *that* all the time?"

As Julie agreed, Daniel strode out of the office with Steven Needlemeyer behind him. "Make an appointment with Missy as soon as you're ready to make concrete plans."

"I have to get the ship out of the mud first."

The builder shook his head in wonder. "A steamship in a farmer's field. You just never know." Then he turned to smile at Julie. "I hope Missy has kept you company. I know all the construction talk can be dull."

Julie managed a giggle. "I did enjoy the girl talk more."

Daniel gave her such a look of shock that she almost kicked him in the shin to keep him from giving her act away. Instead, she looped an arm through his and pouted. "Let's go, Daniel. You promised me some shopping."

"Right."

They walked out, and he cocked an eyebrow at her. "You didn't happen to take a nap around any alien pods?"

"I wasn't body-snatched," she said. "I was acting. I didn't want Needlemeyer asking Missy about our chat. It's better if I looked a little brainless." She went on to tell Daniel about the connection between Needlemeyer and Cantor.

Daniel confirmed what she said. "I complimented a photo of a woman on Needlemeyer's desk and found out it was Elizabeth Cantor. Though Needlemeyer didn't do any name calling, when I mentioned that I knew a lawyer by that name, I could tell there was no love lost between them. They don't strike me as cozy conspirators."

"Me either. I think we can tentatively strike Needlemeyer

off the list. I wish someone would pop up who looked a little more suspicious. Though with two people off the list, we know S-E-N is either Cantor's uncle or a state senator. And we have two senators to choose from." Julie smiled slightly and added, "I always did want to go into politics."

THIRTEEN

Julie could hear the sound of angry voices as soon as she stepped onto the porch of the inn. She peeked through the door. A dozen women crowded around the front desk. She turned to look over her shoulder at Daniel. "Apparently I missed a crisis."

"I would guess the crises usually start when you get there."

Julie opened the door and headed for the desk. The women were all guests, and five of them were part of the same quilting club. She'd pegged the young, tall woman who always wore a scarf as the leader of that club on the day they checked in. Now the young woman clearly had extended that leadership to include almost all the inn's guests as they badgered Shirley at the desk.

The woman began shouting at Julie as soon as she reached them. "What are you going to do about this?"

"Considering I'm not at all sure what 'this' is," Julie said, "I'll need more information before I can answer that."

Everyone began to talk at once. In the swirl of sound, Julie sorted through what words she could make out and realized they thought the inn was harboring a murderer.

Julie held out her hand, stroking the air in front of her like a cat that needed calming. "I assure you, the inn is *not* harboring a murderer."

A gray-haired woman with the taut face of someone in chronic pain pointed toward Daniel as he tried to slink past. "That's him right there!"

Julie frowned. "Mr. Franklin is no murderer."

"He's no quilter either!"

Julie looked around, trying to catch sight of who had shouted the last remark. It sounded familiar. She couldn't make out who it might have been. Everyone seemed to be shouting except Shirley. She was practically draped over the front counter, looking very relieved to be off the hot seat.

"You let someone stay here who wasn't a quilter?" This came from the hipster in the scarf and glasses.

"Mr. Franklin is a historian who specializes in traditional crafts," Julie said. "So although he isn't a quilter, he is a quilt enthusiast." She saw Daniel wince at the description.

"We don't care what his hobbies might be. We're not staying under the same roof with a murderer," the woman said, then looked around her crowd of supporters. "Are we?"

Most of the responses were less loud and less strident, but no less negative. Julie heard more muttered fretting about being "killed in my sleep." She looked around helplessly. She had no idea how to convince them that Daniel wasn't a killer.

"I'm ashamed of you all," Julie said, putting her hands on her hips. "What happened to innocent until proven guilty?"

The hipster quilter matched her stance and her height. "We don't want the man hanged; we just want him out of here."

Julie jumped when a hand rested on her shoulder. Daniel's deep voice cut through the muttering. "I'm not a murderer. The man who died was my best friend in the world, and I'm grieving for him. I would never have hurt George, and I don't know who killed him." The muttering began again, and Daniel raised a finger, asking for one more moment. "But it certainly seems that his death might be related to our work on the excavation. And since I'm also part of that work, I wouldn't want the killer coming here looking for me. I don't want to endanger anyone. I simply hadn't considered that possibility. I'll pay up and leave right now."

"Good!" the hipster snapped. No one else joined her vindictive response. In fact, some of the other quilters looked duly chagrinned.

Julie didn't like giving in to the imaginary fears of the demanding group, but Daniel clearly wasn't going to be talked out of leaving. As he trudged upstairs to pack, Julie turned back to the group.

The leader demanded to know if the inn would be secure after he left. "Maybe you could get the newspaper to print an announcement that he's not here anymore," she suggested.

"I don't think that will be necessary." To Julie's relief, the other women dropped that idea. Her entourage didn't seem to feel Julie had to go that far, though they were clearly a little nervous.

One tiny elderly woman touched Julie's arm. "I really don't believe that young man hurt anyone," she said in a near whisper. "But do you think the murderer might come here looking for him?"

"I don't believe you have anything to worry about," Julie assured her. "The death happened on the Winkler farm, many miles from here."

The woman blinked at her but seemed mollified. Julie calmed everyone's fears and encouraged the ladies to have a complimentary cup of tea in the tea shop. The group dutifully followed Shirley like a flock of fretful ducks. Julie barely had a chance to catch her breath before Daniel was back, ready to check out.

Julie frowned over the paperwork. "I don't like giving in to this kind of thing."

He dropped his battered duffle bag on the floor. "They're scared. That's understandable."

Julie disagreed, but she didn't bother arguing. "Will you tell me where you end up staying?"

"I already know. I called Joe Winkler when I was upstairs. I'll be staying at the farm."

"Even though the excavation is still a crime scene?"

"It won't always be. And I'd like to be close enough to keep an eye on it." He rubbed his face. "This excavation was supposed to be a big adventure. And now my big adventure ..." He laughed without mirth. "*The Grand Adventure* has gotten my best friend killed."

"The only person to blame for this is the murderer," Julie said.

"I know that intellectually. But I don't feel it."

Julie didn't have any words for that. She made him promise to be careful. When he left, she snuck off to the kitchen to get a quiet cup of coffee. She wanted to give Hannah the basket she'd bought and see *someone* be happy with her. She found her friend rummaging through her spice rack and making a list.

"Cooking something special?"

"Not with these," Hannah said. "You've hunted antiques that were younger than some of these spices. I'm replacing them a little at a time; spices are expensive, especially the more exotic ones."

"Well, I have something to take your mind off them." Julie set the beautiful basket on the counter. "Lila Huff is a basket maker, not a killer."

Hannah was delighted with the basket as she turned it over and enthused about the craftsmanship. Then she looked up at Julie. "How come you look so down? You couldn't expect to find the killer on your first attempt to rattle the suspects."

"It would have been nice," Julie said as she brewed a cup of coffee. "But the real problem is that apparently the guests here feel they've discovered the murderer, and it's Daniel." She went on to describe the scene she'd come back to.

Hannah was properly consoling about Daniel. "Once this group checks out at the end of the week, you can always let him come back."

Julie looked down into her coffee mug where the coffee reminded her of her mood, dark and swirling. "You know, it's weird … I thought I recognized the voice of one of the shouters in the group."

"I imagine you've heard them all talk since you checked them in," Hannah said mildly as she slipped a cloth into the basket and set it with the other containers she used for morning muffins.

Julie shook her head. "No, somehow it felt out of place."

"You have a vivid imagination."

"Thanks, pal."

"You'll be thanking me for sure in a moment." Hannah walked back to the desk in the far corner of the kitchen and brought back a thick handful of papers. She gave them to Julie. "I felt a little bit bad about not helping you research your suspects. So when I finished up with breakfast, I spent some time tracking down information."

Julie leafed through the papers. "Anything jump out at you?"

"No, sorry. There's nothing I could find that ties any of them to the Straussberg area in any significant way. Also, no ties to treasure hunting or the steamboat captain's family. You know, I actually found a family tree for the captain online. Apparently his descendants are very proud to have a steamship captain in the family."

"And none of our suspects are his descendants?"

"Definitely not. So I can't point you to the most likely

suspect, but I can point you to the *least* likely."

Julie looked up. "Who's that?"

"Cantor's uncle," Hannah said. "He lives in a pricey assisted-living facility in Jefferson City. The place specializes in Alzheimer's care. Since Alzheimer's patients tend to be wanderers, I imagine they keep close track of their old folks. I doubt the old man was wandering around Winkler Farm."

"Maybe not," Julie said. "But the frustration from the disease has led to some violent behavior when the patients are in good physical shape. Do you know how old the man is?"

"In his early seventies. He's apparently the younger brother to Cantor's father."

"A man that age wouldn't have to be feeble, especially if he was active all his life."

"Still, they're also not going to let him gallivant around loose. That place is pricey. They don't want upset relatives with lost residents."

"You're probably right. He's not a very likely suspect." Julie tapped the papers against her hand. "I'm confident in clearing the two we talked with today too. So that leaves the senators."

"I called their offices."

"You did?"

"I told you, I felt guilty. I said I was doing a feature piece on them and on their ties to the state—family ties, history, etc. I asked about places that were special."

"And?"

"I didn't get to speak to the actual senators, but the staff that answered my questions didn't bring up Straussberg. And they didn't give me anything that tied into this area specifically, other than the fact that Senator Lucas North's brother owns a vineyard and winery in the Missouri wine country. But it's not in Straussberg. It's in Hermann."

Julie sighed. "So North could be tied to the general wine country, but Parson's wife specifically came here to discuss booking a fundraiser."

"You still think she was scoping out the treasure hunting?"

Julie shrugged. "I don't know; it's a reach. And she didn't *seem* to be, but it's awfully coincidental."

"Sometimes a fundraiser is just a fundraiser."

Before Julie could reply, Hannah's phone rang. She held up a finger at Julie and answered the phone. Her expression immediately turned odd, somewhere between annoyance and alarm. She finally put the phone on speaker as a deep, gravelly voice intoned, "Mind your own business, Miss Marks, if you don't want to end up floating down the Missouri without a boat."

FOURTEEN

A chill slipped through her despite the warmth of the kitchen, and Julie shuddered. Then she heard soft static, and the voice repeated the message.

"A recording."

"And a cheery one," Hannah said as she shut off the message. "I finally got my very own death threat. I was feeling left out."

Julie smiled. "Actually, getting a death threat means someone you reached out to is probably connected to the killer! If it were either of the two Daniel and I visited, the death threat would have been to me." Julie rubbed her hands together excitedly. "We're making progress."

"I'm so glad my death threat is the highlight of your day, but keep in mind that I called the nursing home and both senators' offices," Hannah said. "That doesn't narrow it down much. *Are* you ruling out the uncle?"

"Not completely, but he's definitely on the back burner. We have two front-runners—the senators."

"Unless the killer is the lawyer," Hannah said. "The nursing home could have clued him in to my calls about his uncle."

Julie tapped her nails against the counter as she thought about that. "I think we'll start with the senators, but it's possible we'll need to pay a visit to the nursing home. If it is the lawyer, that should shake him up."

"Wonderful," Hannah said flatly. She tapped the pile of pages she'd given Julie. "You should read this stuff. You might find something I've missed. You might even want to have Daniel read them."

Julie gulped the last of her coffee and gathered up the papers. "I'll take them to the front desk and spend a few hours reading."

Unfortunately, she found Inga waiting for her at the front desk. "I was cleaning the blue suite, and I noticed there is a problem in the bathroom."

"What kind of problem?"

"With the ..." Inga dropped her voice to a whisper, " ... commode."

"What kind of problem?"

The older woman looked as if any discussion of bathroom fixtures were almost too distasteful to stand, but she finally managed to whisper, "It's running."

"Did you jiggle the handle?"

Inga managed to look both offended and scandalized at the same time. "Of course, but I don't think we should be discussing this out here. I clean the rooms, but I'm not a plumber. You should go look at it."

Julie sighed and dumped the printouts at the front desk. She grabbed the small toolbox she kept there and followed Inga's stiff figure up the stairs. The plumbing problem proved to be well within her skill set, but it seemed to be the beginning of a chain reaction of issues that kept her busy all the way until it was time to lock up for the night. Having missed supper, Julie made herself a sandwich in the empty kitchen—even Hannah had gotten to bed before her—and carried it up to the third floor.

Julie sat in her favorite chair by the gas fireplace and put her feet up with a contented sigh. She took a bite of the sandwich made with Hannah's amazing chicken salad. The tender chicken and crisp bites of celery blended perfectly with the sweet dried cranberries Hannah always added for color.

It almost made up for the tough afternoon.

When her phone rang, she glared at it for a moment. She hated to set the sandwich aside, but she glanced at the I.D. and saw it was Daniel. She spoke through a mouth half-full of chicken. "How's the farm?"

"It's good. I'm staying in the old farmhand quarters, which seems to be where all the stuff that the Winklers aren't sure what to do with ends up. It's crowded but not uncomfortable—a little like sleeping in the middle of a yard sale. But your voice sounds funny. You're not coming down sick, are you?"

"No, sorry. I'm eating." She set her sandwich aside and told him about the information Hannah had dug up—and about the phone threat.

"I don't like this," Daniel said.

"I do. It means Hannah is on the right track. *We're* on the right track. I'm thinking it's one of the senators. Though we can't rule out Cantor. He might have heard about Hannah's call to his uncle's nursing home. Still, I think that's a long shot."

"I'm not sure I'd consider Cantor a long shot. He seems like exactly the type who would threaten a woman, but I don't like that threats are coming in at the inn, and I'm stuck way out here."

"I think we can look after ourselves," Julie said. *It's not like we've never been threatened before.* Julie didn't say the last bit aloud since it would bring up questions she didn't want to answer.

Daniel huffed, but he didn't argue. "Did Hannah dig up a connection between *any* of our suspects and *The Grand Adventure*?"

"No, though I haven't read everything she printed out." She glanced around her room, then realized she'd left the printouts downstairs on the front desk. She yawned and wondered if it was worth going down to get them.

"There must be some kind of connection, although I can't imagine how a pre–Civil War shipwreck could provoke a twenty-first–century murder."

Murder, Julie thought. What kinds of things normally provoked murder? Money, of course, but also secrets. "What if someone is trying to cover up a secret that has nothing to do with the ship? What if it has to do with Winkler Farm?"

"The farm? They grow organic food. How could that incite someone to commit murder?"

"Not the farming, the land. What if someone is worried about what might get dug up on the Winkler farm?" Julie asked. "Something other than the wreck?"

"Like what?"

"I don't know … like a dead body. Maybe one that hasn't been in the ground for over a hundred years."

"It's a theory, I suppose. I guess it makes more sense than killing someone over a steamboat wreck." Daniel paused for a moment, and Julie listened to the slight fuzzy sound of the open line. "I have an idea. I know a woman in Tennessee who trains cadaver dogs. I could have her come out and search the site. If the dog senses human remains, we'll call the police."

Julie felt a surge of excitement. "That's a fantastic plan!" If they happened to find a *recent* dead body, that would change everything about the investigation.

They chatted for a few more minutes until Julie managed to yawn into the phone for the third time.

Daniel must have heard it. "You sound tired, and I'm keeping you up. I guess I found it a little lonelier out in this bunkhouse than I expected. You go to sleep. I'll call my friend in the morning and tell you what she says."

"Great." Julie yawned the end of the word and hung up. She thought again about going down to collect the printouts and spend some time reading them, but she couldn't muster enough energy. Instead, she headed for bed.

Daniel's friend couldn't make it out to the farm for several days, which was fine with Julie. A new quilting group checked in and were afire with questions about the area attractions. They also bought lots of things at the tea-and-quilt shop, so Julie knew Millie would be pleased. She received another interesting postcard from the owner. The photo on this one featured a cave and people in spelunking gear. Millie's note said she'd be coming back to the inn soon.

"'Soon' is a little nonspecific," Julie told the postcard before slipping it into her blazer pocket and allowing a guest to drag her into the quilt shop to give an opinion on fabric choices for the woman's quilt.

As things calmed down at the inn, Julie found herself restless. Waiting for a cadaver dog felt like giving the murderer too much time to work out another plan of attack. She needed to be doing something. She considered reading through the papers Hannah had given her. Still, reading wasn't action. She needed to *do* something.

She put Shirley in charge, grabbed Hannah from the kitchen, and headed to the Missouri Hills Care Center. "This might let us mark one name completely off the list," Julie said. "That would make me feel like we were accomplishing something."

"Fine with me," Hannah answered agreeably as she hopped into the car. "I could use a short break from the kitchen."

The nursing home was beautiful with lush, expansive grounds. They climbed out of the car, and Hannah spotted a gardener working on a nearby hedge. "I think I'll go ask questions about how easy it would be to get out of this place. I'll meet you at the car when you're done."

"Divide and conquer," Julie said. She headed through the arched entry and crossed the marble floor to the front desk. When she complimented the place, the receptionist brightened. "This was an old estate many years ago." She dropped her voice slightly to add, "It's the most beautiful place I've ever worked. Usually nursing home buildings look as worn as the residents."

"No doubt." Julie explained that she wanted to visit Maxwell Cantor Sr. and the receptionist's smile faded slightly.

"You'll need an escort back to that wing," the receptionist said. "And you'll have to speak with the head nurse there to be sure Mr. Cantor is up to visitors today." As she was speaking, a girl who looked as if she couldn't be out of high school came through with an armload of towels. The receptionist called out to her. "Izzy, please, take this lady to the closed wing and introduce her to Nurse Sinclair."

The teenager nodded briskly and asked Julie to follow her. As soon as they were out of hearing of the front desk, the girl asked, "You visiting a relative?"

"Family friend," Julie said.

"Be prepared. Your friend might not know you," Izzy said.

Julie managed to look sad about that. "Does that happen a lot?"

"The folks in this unit have their good days and their bad days," Izzy said. "Usually they're sweet, but sometimes— watch out!"

"What do you mean by that?" Julie asked.

Izzy dropped her voice still more, and Julie had to lean close to the teen to hear. "One of the old guys popped Nurse Sinclair smack in the eye when she wouldn't let him go for a walk."

"Oh my!" Julie said. "That wasn't dear old Max, was it?"

"No, but Max has his moments. He broke a volunteer's hand one day. I won't work in that unit at all, and they *pay* me. Anyway, Max has other skills."

"Like what?" Julie asked.

"They call him 'Houdini.' He's always getting outside. The old guy's pretty slick, considering he doesn't know where he is half the time." A panicky look crossed the teenager's face. "Look, I'm not supposed to talk about the residents like that. I didn't mean anything. Don't turn me in, OK? I need this job so I can save enough money to go to college next year."

"I won't tell," Julie said. She would have pumped the girl for more information, but they had reached the doors to the unit, and the teenager had grown very quiet and formal. She handed Julie off to the head nurse.

"Max is one of our favorites," the nurse said. "And he's having a good day."

She led Julie to a beautifully decorated room with tall windows and lots of light. It didn't look anything like a hospital room. It didn't even have a hospital bed. Maxwell Cantor Senior looked up as they entered.

"Hi, Max," Julie said. "I thought I would come by for a visit."

His forehead creased as he squinted at her. "Do I know you?"

"It's Julie," she said, feeling guilty for adding to the old man's confusion.

He shook his head sadly. "I used to be so good with names and faces. I don't remember you, but I'll never turn away a pretty girl."

Julie sat in the chair beside Max, and the nurse slipped away. "You don't actually know me, Max. So you didn't forget."

He smiled. "That's a relief. So Julie-whom-I-don't-know, what can I do for you?"

"I live over in Straussberg. Do you know the town?"

He thought about it a moment, then nodded. "I have a nephew who lives there. I haven't visited. He's a vile little beast. My sister-in-law spoiled him rotten."

"I've met him."

"Sorry."

"Are you familiar with a farm in that area? The Winkler farm? Or with an old Civil War steamboat wreck? The ship was called *The Grand Adventure*."

The old man shook his head. "No. I was dreadful at history in school. I was too busy teasing the pretty girls. Should I know anything about it?"

"Your nephew tried to buy the farm," Julie said. "I wondered why."

"If it was my nephew, it was probably for nothing good." He shook his head sadly, then his gaze turned toward the tall windows, and he became very still.

"Mr. Cantor?" Julie said after a moment.

He turned back to her in surprise. "Hello. Are you new? Can you take me outside?"

"I'm sorry, I can't."

He frowned. "I want to go outside."

"Let me go get one of the nurses. Maybe she can take you." Julie began to rise but Max grabbed her arm.

"I want to go out. Take me out of here."

"Max, please, let go of my arm."

"I want to go out!" Max's voice rose to a shout. Nurses hurried in then, and with the rush of new people, Max let go of her. She slipped out of the room, rubbing her arm. Max's grip was definitely strong.

When she got outside, she found Hannah leaning against the car. They climbed in and Hannah asked her what she'd learned. "I learned Max is considered the Houdini of the facility," Julie said. "And he's certainly strong enough to hurt someone."

"Max isn't the only Houdini here," Hannah said. "According to the gardener, they misplace residents regularly. They usually track them down on the grounds, but a few have made it out onto the road and even into town."

"Was Max one of those few?"

"He didn't know any names."

Julie thought about it as they drove back to the inn. Max was definitely a sweet old man when he was lucid, but she didn't doubt that he had the strength to hurt someone. But why would he go all the way to the Winkler farm? Why go after George?

"He still doesn't make sense as a suspect," Julie said finally.

Hannah sighed as she stretched out her short legs in the seat. "None of them do."

Julie had to agree. None of them did. There had to be something they weren't seeing.

On the day of the search with the cadaver dog, Julie talked Hannah into covering for her so she could watch the happenings at the excavation site. When she reached it, she was surprised to see a small crowd, including several police officers, watching a white German shepherd roam over the area. Julie asked Daniel about the police when she reached his side.

"Kara does a lot of work for police departments," Daniel

said. "So she didn't want to annoy the local cops by nosing around a crime scene without permission. Thus ..." He gestured toward the police officers.

Julie nodded toward Detective Frost. "He looks cheery."

"I'm not sure that man's face knows what cheery feels like."

The detective seemed to feel their eyes on him. He turned away from the woman with the dog and walked across the pitted ground toward them. "Miss Ellis." He wagged a finger at her. "You let me believe you were Millie Rogers."

"Did I?" Julie asked. "That was such a horrible and confusing night." She pointedly turned her attention away to watch the dog.

"I don't expect this to produce anything," Frost said. "But I didn't see how it could hurt either. I'm sure we'll find that the murder and the murderer are less mysterious."

"As long as you find him," Daniel said.

The detective turned to give Daniel a long, level stare. "We will."

Julie was impressed with the careful way Daniel's friend worked the area with her dog. The big white dog covered the area with focused attention, his nose to the ground. Occasionally he would look over at the slim, athletic woman who held his leash and watched his every move.

"I've never seen a cadaver dog," Julie whispered to Daniel.

It was Frost who turned to her and said, "I have, though I've never worked with this one. You'd think all the smells on a farm would be a distraction, but cadaver dogs seem to be able to cut right through them."

Still, for all the care the team of woman and dog put into the search, nothing caught the dog's interest. Finally the woman clipped the lead back on the German shepherd and walked over to Daniel. "If there's a body buried here, it's in something airtight."

"Thanks for trying, Kara. It was probably a long shot."

"What if the body was buried a long time ago?" Julie asked. "Ten or twenty years?"

"It doesn't matter," Kara said. "Chase is trained to find everything from fresh remains to old bones." Then she smiled. "Not that I understand how he does it. The scientists are still trying to figure it out. When Chase was getting his training, they told me there are 480 different compounds that give off scent in a decaying body."

"That's amazing." Julie looked at the dog admiringly. He gave her an open-mouthed grin with his tongue lolled out and offered a paw.

Kara patted his head. "He likes you."

"Is it all right if I pet him?" Julie asked. "I know you're not supposed to pet dogs when they're working."

"He's off duty."

Julie scratched the German shepherd's velvety ears and was rewarded by the dog leaning heavily against her leg.

"I'm going to get going—unless you have some other location for me to check?"

"No, this was it." Daniel's voice was gloomy. "Thanks for coming out."

"You know I'd do anything to help with finding George's killer," Kara said, shaking her head. "I hadn't seen him in a few years, but I can still hear his off-key, made-up songs. He was one of a kind."

Daniel nodded. "He was that."

As they were saying their goodbyes, Detective Frost took Julie's arm and pulled her aside. "You seem to be a level-headed woman, but you need to be careful."

"Careful of what?" Julie asked.

He looked back at Daniel. "I know women like the whole Indiana Jones thing."

"Oh?" Julie asked tightly.

The detective's face turned even grimmer. "I believe Mr. Franklin is more Hannibal Lecter than Indiana Jones. Remember, charming doesn't always mean trustworthy—or even sane."

"As much as I enjoy hearing you slander my friend," Julie said, "I'm going to have to ask you to let go of my arm. I need to go back to work."

"Don't be charmed into a relationship with a murderer, Ms. Ellis. I'd hate to see you become the next victim of an unfortunate *accident* around Daniel Franklin."

FIFTEEN

Depressed, frustrated, and annoyed, Julie headed back to the inn. Rather than risk bumping into guests while in a foul mood, she walked around the neatly tended kitchen garden at the back of the inn. The rows of herbs were dying back from the cold nights, but they still reflected the nearly military straight rows they'd grown in.

The vegetables were equally bare, except for a few pumpkins. Julie stared at them and wondered if she should have some kind of pumpkin-carving event at the end of October. She'd seen some amazing pumpkin carvers on television and knew it was becoming an art form. It might be interesting. At the very least, she should look into getting a carver to do a couple quilt-theme pumpkins for the porch.

"I hope you don't have designs on my pumpkins."

Julie turned to see Hannah grinning at her from the small back porch and replied, "Not yours, but I might pick some up to be carved when I'm out at the Winkler farm again." She looked around the garden again. "You have a real knack for gardening."

Hannah hooted. "Not me! This is Inga's work. My idea of gardening would involve tossing the seeds on the ground and letting them fend for themselves. I'm surprised you didn't recognize the perfectly square corners on the garden beds."

"They're certainly neat," Julie said. "But I couldn't picture Inga getting dirty."

"The dirt is probably afraid to stick to her. How did the cadaver hunt go?"

Julie shook her head. "It didn't include any cadavers, but

I did get a warning from the homicide detective. He thinks Daniel is some kind of Jekyll-and-Hyde character."

"That's a charming thought. Come on in the kitchen; I have a present for you."

Julie followed her friend, and Hannah handed her another small pile of papers. "I did some more research on the senators. This is personal stuff including public appearances and campaign rumors. I even printed message board posts. Anywhere gossip lived, I tracked it down."

Julie shuffled through the stack, acutely aware that she had barely skimmed the last pile of papers Hannah had given her. She'd have to be more diligent this time. "Did you turn up anything interesting?"

"Not on Senator Parson. The man has a record so clean you could eat from it, and that's astoundingly rare in politics. He had apparently even kept most of his campaign promises. One of them involved help for small farms in danger of bankruptcy. It saved a lot of old family farms and a few vineyards that were hit hard when the economy took a big hit. According to his bio, he has three clergymen in his family tree."

"So he's a saint?"

Hannah shrugged. "He's a politician. Still, he seems like one of the better ones. There's a rumor that he has his eye on the big leagues in Washington, D.C."

"Don't they all? I still find it odd timing that his wife came here," Julie said. "It's suspicious."

"But not out of character for this guy. He's big on connections with the everyday working man. So if he were going to have a fundraiser, he'd surely pick someplace like this. It fits his past behavior."

"OK, fine. He's swell," Julie said. "Tell me about Senator Lucas North."

"He's pretty much everything Parson's not. He's a woman-izer for sure, and I'm amazed his wife is still with him. One interesting thing, though."

"What's that?"

"During his campaign, there was talk that he might have been having a relationship with one of his aides. It was never confirmed. The girl left the campaign when she was hurt badly during a mugging. She almost died."

Julie quirked an eyebrow. "You think he might have a history of getting rid of people who get in his way?"

"I don't know. She might simply have been mugged. It does happen. And she didn't die."

"Maybe we should talk to her."

"I'll see if I can track her down."

"Did you turn up any connections between these guys and Straussberg?"

Hannah shook her head. "Some of their policy decisions have affected folks in this area, but there's no clear connec-tion. Since Daniel comes from money, I even looked into a possible connection between his family money and campaign funding. I didn't find anything, though tracking campaign funding is tricky."

"Which one of the senators would *you* check out first?"

"Probably North. He's not a good guy."

Julie nodded. "I'll take a run up to Jefferson City tomor-row and see if I can get in to speak to them."

"I thought you might want to do that, so I got you some credentials. There's a Constance Platt with *American Farm Family* magazine. Both of these guys are courting farmers hard, though Parson does a better job of it. Pretend you want to do a feature. That should get you in."

Julie thanked her friend and headed for the front desk.

She began leafing through the papers while she pulled her phone from her pocket to call Daniel. Before she could dial, Shirley bustled out of the tearoom, clutching a book. Julie waited with the phone in her hand.

"How did the search go?" Shirley asked.

"The search?"

"For the dead bodies on Winkler Farm."

"You knew about that?"

Shirley gave her a pitying look. "Everyone knew about that."

"No bodies."

"Oh, that's too bad." Shirley plunked down the book on the desk in front of her.

Julie glanced at it. The title read *Horrible Happenings on the Missouri*. "Working on another Stories and Stitches night?"

"No, this one is for you," Shirley said. "There's a whole chapter on *The Grand Adventure* with lots of inside stories. Though one of the stories claims that *The Grand Adventure* was smuggling slaves to the free state of Iowa. The slaves were hidden down in the engine room. That theory says the ship was sunk by slave hunters, and the slaves all drowned."

"If that were true, the dog would have alerted," Julie countered. "The handler was sure that the dog could detect a body through anything that wasn't airtight."

Shirley frowned. "Maybe they were hidden in the boiler. That might have been airtight."

"Smuggling living, breathing people in an airtight container doesn't sound terribly practical," Julie pointed out. "Plus, I'm pretty sure the ship would have needed the boiler to be full of water, not people."

"It doesn't matter. There are other stories in there. One of them might have some bearing on this situation. You should read it."

The little woman was so earnest that Julie didn't have the heart to resist, even though she wasn't sure where she'd fit in time to do more reading. "Thanks. I will."

Shirley beamed. "I'm glad. I've been feeling bad about your young man having to leave the inn. I thought maybe my stories might have played a part, so I wanted to do something to help."

"That's very nice of you." Julie waved her phone slightly. "I was about to call Daniel. I'll tell him about the book."

"Excellent. Do tell him I wish him well. I'd better get back to the tearoom now. I left two ladies debating over quilt patterns." She hurried away and Julie dialed the phone.

"Julie!" Daniel's voice boomed at her. "I have fantastic news."

"Really?"

"The police have released the scene. I can get back to work tomorrow."

"I'm so glad."

They chatted about Daniel's plans for his workday, and Julie couldn't imagine trying to pull him away from his work to interview the senators. She'd simply go by herself to see them in the morning. Since she didn't want to drive to Jefferson City for nothing, she called ahead to each of the senator's offices with the story Hannah had suggested.

"Senator North won't be in his office tomorrow," a harried-sounding woman told her. "He's speaking at a civic group luncheon, but I believe I can squeeze in a chat for you if you don't mind meeting him at the venue before it begins."

"I don't mind." Julie took down the address. *One down, one to go.*

Senator Parson was tougher. Apparently his schedule was packed, and no one wanted to make any promises about connecting with him.

"I understand," Julie said to his assistant. "But I have an interview set with Senator North, and I hoped to include some mention of Senator Parson as well. He's worked so much harder for farmers."

"You're speaking with Senator North?" the man's voice slipped into a high tenor. "I'm certain we can find some time for Senator Parson to meet with you. Can you be at the State Capitol around one? The senator likes to eat by the fountain on the north side of the building on sunny days. I'm sure he could squeeze in a moment."

"You want me to interview him while he's eating?"

"If you don't catch him then, I'm not sure when you will. You can't miss the fountain. It's the one with the squirting fish and the strange horse thing. Honestly, I sometimes think I'll never understand art, but the senator loves it."

"I'll be there."

After breakfast, Julie twisted her hair into a bun, grabbed her camera, and dressed in her most conservative skirt and blouse. She looked herself over in the mirror and decided she looked sufficiently journalistic.

The drive to Jefferson City was overcast. Julie hoped the clouds would clear so that she could catch Senator Parson at the fountain later. The gray sky softened the autumn colors around her, and she found the change lovely. *I'd like those colors in my room,* she thought. *I really should begin a quilt of my own.* It had been years since she'd quilted, but being surrounded by so many people at the inn who truly loved the craft made her increasingly itchy to pick a project.

In her head, she matched each color around her to a specific fabric she'd seen in the inn's quilt-and-tea shop. It helped make the drive go more quickly, and soon she was in Jefferson City. Though the city was mostly laid out in neat, straight lines, she was happy to have the help of electronic navigation.

"How did we get along with nothing but paper maps for so long?" she asked the small device. Not surprisingly, it had no answer.

She finally reached the trendy restaurant downtown about a half hour before her appointment.

The early bird gets the worm, she thought as she grabbed the camera from the backseat. *And this guy sounds like quite a worm.*

When she asked about the senator's group at the hostess stand, she was directed upstairs to the private dining room. The senator was perched on a stool at the small bar at the end of the room. He was sipping amber liquid that she suspected wasn't tea. His suit, artfully rumpled hair, casual pose, and glass in his hand made him look like a magazine advertisement for success.

"Senator," she said offering her best professional smile. "Constance Platt, *American Farm Families.*"

The senator's face lit up. "Well, you're certainly not what I was expecting."

"Oh? How's that?"

He laughed. "You know. With a name like *American Farm Families*, I was expecting a sturdy country girl, not a hot gal like you."

At forty, Julie considered herself neither a girl nor a gal, but she didn't think he'd appreciate the distinction. She tried for a smile, though it felt more like a grimace. "I'm grateful to you for carving out some time to chat with me."

"I'm just sorry I didn't carve out more." He patted the barstool beside him. "What did you want to ask me?"

She skipped the stool he patted and took the next

one. It seemed wise to keep at least one piece of furniture between them. "We want a feature that makes you feel more approachable."

His smile was positively oily. "I am *very* approachable."

"I meant to our readers." Again she offered her tight smile. "It would help if I highlight your ties to our area. We sell especially well in Missouri wine country. Do you have any connections to that area?"

He shrugged. "I like wine. Does that count?"

"That might earn you a few brownie points. But what about family? Do you have any there? Or stories of happy visits or vacations to, say, Straussberg? Perhaps you own land or businesses in the area?"

"Sorry, no." He took a deep drink from his glass. "My brother owns a winery in Hermann, but I've never been out there. I don't spend a lot of time in the country. But if you think it will help the article, I can drive out to Bill's vineyard for a photo shoot. Or I can buy apples from a farmer's market. Something like that."

"We can probably arrange for something like that," she agreed. "Maybe we can find a farm stand in Straussberg."

Senator North laughed. "Is that your hometown? You seem in a big hurry to get me out there." He leaned forward far enough to lay a hand on her knee. Julie removed it and put it on the empty stool between them.

She narrowed her eyes as she considered what to ask next. "Are you interested in state history? Many of our readers love nostalgia and history pieces. A tie to state history would also help humanize you."

"History? You mean like the whole Louisiana Purchase thing? No." He laughed. "In fact, my idea of a *real* museum would be the National Sporting Arms Museum in Springfield.

That's about the only time I'm out of the city—when I go hunting."

"Hunting?"

The senator leaned in a little too close again. "I thought that might perk you up. I know how women like men with big guns. I could show you my rifle."

"No thanks," she said quickly. "But I am curious. Do you go hunting in any of the areas around the Missouri River?"

He shook his head. "I have a hunting cabin in Alaska. I fly up every year and shoot caribou. Wait, I have a picture." He pulled out his wallet and showed her a photo of him standing with one booted foot planted on the shoulder of a dead caribou. "Gorgeous, isn't it?"

"It was."

"You aren't one of those Bambi lovers, are you? I'd be really disappointed."

"Actually I think we're done here," Julie said as she slid off the barstool. She needed to get away from the man before she slapped him on general principle. "I'll call your office about that photo shoot."

"Hey, what's your hurry?" The senator stood and grabbed her arm. "I didn't even get your card in case I want to call you."

Julie pulled but the man didn't let go, so she took a sharp step back, bringing the heel of her shoe down on his instep at the same time that she let him pull on her arm, snapping it backward sharply into the man's stomach. His yelp when she stepped on his foot turned wheezy when her elbow connected with his stomach.

"Oh, I'm so sorry," Julie said. "I didn't mean to stumble into you. Thanks for the chat." She spun and hurried from the room.

She was out of the lot and driving down the street before

she noticed her hands were shaking. She decided to stop and have a quiet cup of coffee to regroup. Otherwise her reaction to the first senator was likely to cloud her judgment about the second one.

It didn't appear that Senator North had any interest in a shipwreck in Straussberg, but his love of guns was possibly worth considering. Julie sighed in frustration. What if Senator Parson wasn't interested in the shipwreck either? Where would that leave her investigation? She had a handful of people who might be distantly suspicious, but no clear prime suspect. The treasure hunt was back on, and since they didn't know who killed George, Daniel might well be in danger at the site. She was surprised at how upset she felt about that notion. She couldn't deny that she was forming some kind of personal attachment to Daniel Franklin. With her history of walking quickly, if not running, from all romantic entanglements, she found it upsetting that she might already be entangled.

SIXTEEN

As she expected, Julie had a bit of a hike from the parking lot to the fountain at the Capitol building. She walked by a group of schoolchildren who stood fidgeting while their teacher lectured them. One little girl turned to look at Julie with a wide smile. She pointed at the Capitol building and asked, "Isn't it pretty?"

Julie nodded. "Very."

The little girl seemed to take that as an opportunity to chat. "It's special too. I did a report."

Julie looked up at the tall building with its columns and dome. It looked a lot like the U.S. Capitol to her and pretty much exactly what she would have pictured in her mind when she thought of the capitol. "Is that so?"

The child nodded eagerly and switched to a more formal report-giving tone. "The columns don't use the same leaves as classic columns. They used leaves that grow here in Missouri." She dropped her voice. "I got an A on my report."

"Good for you," Julie whispered back.

She saw the teacher's gaze turn to her and decided she should continue on before she got the little girl in trouble for chatting with strangers. She thought about the columns as she walked. She would never have noticed that the leaves were special, because she never would have looked that close. It was so easy to overlook important details. Was she doing that with the case?

When she reached the large fountain on the north side of the building, she didn't see anyone. She stood, looking at the sprays of water jetting from the mouths of stylized fish being held by chubby cherubs. The largest figures in the pond looked like centaurs, but their rear horse legs blended into a long tail like a mermaid. No wonder the staffer had called it a "weird horse thing."

Julie wondered what the attraction was for the senator. Maybe he just liked water. She tilted her head to one side as she studied it. Or he could love fishing. Or maybe he saw himself as a blend of different things, like the centaur figures.

She shrugged and it turned into a shiver; the day was becoming colder and grayer. It certainly wasn't an inviting day to eat outside.

"Miss?"

She turned to face a gangly young man with bad acne. He wore a suit that didn't quite fit, as if he had hopes of growing into it. When she smiled a question at him, he thrust out a folded piece of paper. "From the senator." Then he turned and practically ran for the capitol building.

To her surprise, the note addressed her as "Miss Ellis" instead of by the reporter's name that she'd given the staffer on the phone. The message was short and direct. He knew her cover story of the interview was false and wasn't going to talk with charlatans looking for a scandal. Then he simply signed his name. She stared at the careful penmanship. *How could he possibly know who I am?*

She slipped the note into her blazer pocket and began the short trek back to the car. She wondered if it was significant that Senator Parson had discovered her ruse without even meeting her. Senator North had showed no interest in checking up on her before the meeting. Discovering she wasn't the reporter would be easy enough. All the senator's staff had to do was call the magazine. But how did he know her real name? That was a much more pressing question.

The only person at the capitol likely to know her on sight was the senator's wife. Technically, she might have caught sight of her and stopped the senator on the way to meeting her. It would only have taken a moment to write the note. But the theory still seemed rather far-fetched.

Julie drove back to the coffee shop to do some quiet thinking before heading back to the inn. The chill that had shaken her at the fountain seemed reluctant to go away, and she knew the coffee would warm her up.

She stared into her coffee cup, pondering whether anything that had happened meant something. She felt as if she were staring at a table full of loose puzzle pieces with no idea of how to begin putting them together.

She startled at the scrape of the chair across from her.

Randall Cantor sat down and blocked her view. "I *demand* to know exactly what kind of scandal you're trying to involve so many of my clients in."

She looked at him mildly. "I have no idea what you're talking about."

"You mean you're not the leggy brunette who's visited two state senators, the owner of a construction company, and my sick uncle?"

Julie smiled. "You left out Lila Huff."

His frown darkened into a scowl. "What are you after?"

"You know what I want to know. Who wants the Winkler farm? The answer to that could be the answer to the question of who killed George Benning. Unless, of course, I'm on the wrong trail, and you killed him yourself as a favor to your client."

He pointed an accusing finger at her. "That's slander."

"It's only slander if someone besides you and I hear it,"

Julie said. "You're the one who's getting loud. I'm not interested in scandal, Mr. Cantor. I'm interested in truth. Someone is dead. Hasn't the time passed for keeping secrets?"

"I'm a lawyer. Keeping my clients' secrets is part of my job." He narrowed his eyes. "I'll bet you had something to do with the break-in at my office."

She laughed at him. "I'm an innkeeper. Not a cat burglar."

"Nothing was stolen," Cantor said. "But suddenly you seem to know the names of many of my clients."

"I ask a lot of questions."

"You certainly do."

They glared at each other silently for a moment. Then Julie asked, "Why does Senator Parson want to buy the Winkler farm?"

The lawyer huffed. "The senator's family already owns plenty of property down near the borders of Kentucky and Tennessee. I doubt he needs a farm."

"Maybe he has something against the excavation."

"As far as I can tell, Senator Parson's only interest outside his work is fishing. Now if the excavation endangered fishing in Missouri, it might get him worked up. Otherwise, he's not really the type to go after anyone."

"Senator North certainly seems to have plenty of interests outside of work," Julie said.

The lawyer shook his head. "I'm not going to dig dirt with you. Nor do I have time or interest in discussing the private lives of my clients. None of them has any reason to be interested in your boyfriend's dig."

With that, Cantor stood up.

"What about your uncle? Could one of his wanderings have brought him all the way to Winkler Farm?"

Cantor slammed his hand down on the table, drawing a sharp look from the patrons around them. He spoke through clenched teeth. "My uncle is an old, sick man. Leave him alone."

"He seemed pretty hale and hearty when I met him."

"Stay away from my family and my clients. If even a whiff of scandal comes my way, I will know the source, and I will deal with it."

Julie watched the man stalk off, so angry that it made his gait uneven. She smiled slightly. Her day was looking up. She didn't have any answers, but she was definitely stirring things up. In her experience, the best way to get at the center of any problem was to create ripples along the edges.

On the drive back to the inn, she turned up the radio and tapped the steering wheel in time to the music. She'd chosen the route with the most back roads. She wasn't in any great hurry to get back to the inn, and less traffic gave her more chance to think.

She passed another sprawling farm. Farmland always looked so ragged in the fall when everything was withering in preparation for winter. She wondered if they'd have a lot of snow. She was used to New York City snow. She suspected life was different in the country.

Julie glanced in her rearview mirror and frowned as a dark SUV rushed up behind her, huddling far too close to her bumper.

"The road's practically empty, so go around me," she muttered.

Instead, the SUV continued to tailgate. Julie sped up slightly, uncomfortable with having a vehicle so close behind her. In the countryside, it wasn't uncommon for an animal to dash out into the road, but the car behind her was giving her no option for braking. It would run right over her if she slowed down suddenly.

Julie rolled down her window and the fall chill rushed into the car. She thrust her arm out and gestured for the SUV to pass. It merely rode her bumper. A tickle of nerves started in Julie's stomach.

She picked up speed again, her eyes watching for possible turnoffs. She could duck into one of the farm drives and let the SUV continue on its way. But she'd reached a stretch that didn't offer any options for leaving the road. The shoulders were narrow as well, so if she tried to simply pull off, she'd be driving over someone's withered cornfield.

Time stretched out as Julie searched for a way off the road. Now and then, she'd glance into the mirror. The SUV's dark windows gave her no glimpse of the driver. The anonymity made it all the more ominous.

Julie fought the urge to increase speed again and began slowly to ease off the gas instead. The SUV wasn't going to let her pull ahead, and she didn't dare lose control. Suddenly, the bigger vehicle darted into the left-hand lane and quickly pulled up beside Julie's car.

She let up on the gas to slow down so the SUV could complete the pass. Instead, it matched her deceleration, and they continued to ride side by side. At least they could see far ahead down the straight road, so she didn't have to worry about oncoming traffic. But the emptiness of the road also meant no witnesses for whatever the SUV driver had in mind.

She glanced quickly at the big vehicle. Its dark side window reflected back a blurry copy of her face, and she shuddered at how close the monster was beside her. "Just pass already," she muttered.

The SUV suddenly swerved toward her, as if trying to get in the lane right on top of Julie's car. She pounded the horn just before the two vehicles bumped hard. Her car rocked with the impact, but she kept it on the road.

"You're out of your mind!" she yelled. Her grip on the steering wheel turned her knuckles white from the effort.

The SUV still didn't pass. Again it came over on her, harder this time, shoving the car toward the narrow shoulder. Again she managed to ride out the hit. She was desperate to call 911, but she didn't dare take a hand off the wheel to get her phone. Then the SUV made contact with her again.

This time she couldn't keep her car on the road. She skidded across the narrow shoulder and barreled into the cornfield beyond. Her car bucked and shuddered as it rode over the rough terrain. The dry cornstalks snapped with a sound like broken bones. Finally, the car jerked to a stop. Julie immediately twisted in the seat to see if the driver of the SUV was still coming after her. The road was clear. The driver had obviously sped on.

Julie sat unmoving, her hands still gripping the steering wheel. She tried to calm her breathing. Her heart continued to pound in her ears. She didn't doubt for a moment that the driver of the SUV was the same person who had killed George—and whoever it was, he was definitely marking Julie as a prime target.

Seventeen

The autumn breeze made the dry cornstalks scrape against Julie's car in whispery scratches as she sat inside, waiting for her panic to subside. After a moment, she pushed her door open, shoving over another stalk, and climbed out. She circled the car, keeping one hand on the frame since her legs still felt wobbly. She was surprised to see very little damage done to the car. The cornstalks had gone down without a fight. She was still inspecting the vehicle when a man burst through the corn, startling her.

"Gah!" Julie let out a small shriek.

He froze and held up his hands. "Sorry, lady. I didn't mean to scare you. I saw that SUV run you off the road. I've seen some crazy drivers, but that guy must have been drunk."

"Must have," she said, her voice still as wobbly as her knees.

"I called the cops," he said. "They should be here soon. I didn't see the license of that thing, but I got a real good look at it."

Julie nodded. She hadn't caught the license details either. The farmer's wife pushed through the stalks then and began mothering Julie in earnest. She commanded her husband to wait at the car for the police while she took Julie inside the house and made some hot cocoa. "It's the best thing in the world for shock," she said as she led Julie away.

The cocoa did help, though the round of questions from the police didn't. After years of avoiding police interaction as she skated the fine line between legal and illegal in her business, it was hard to just open up and talk about the threats she and

Hannah had received. She couldn't see the point. What could the police do? It was all so vague. She had no enemies that she could name, especially since she was pretty sure the art theft ring was not driving the back roads of Missouri, hoping to run her into a cornfield. She described the incident and the vehicle, but that's all she offered. The officer diligently took notes, but she could see he didn't have much hope of finding the offender. Black SUVs weren't exactly rare.

The farmer's wife insisted her husband drive the car out of the field and check it over thoroughly before letting Julie back in it. "You don't want to get halfway home and have a breakdown on top of everything else."

Julie agreed. She could tell it would do no good to argue. Eventually she was on the road again, though she was far from completely recovered. Every time a new vehicle came over a rise in the road, Julie felt a jolt of fear. She was grateful to finally reach Straussberg and the inn.

To her surprise, she found the owner, Millie Rogers, standing at the front desk when she walked in. Julie's smile at the older woman was not returned.

"What's this business about murderers staying at the inn?" Millie asked sharply.

So much for pleasantries. Julie's smile darkened. "We haven't had any murderers staying at the inn."

"That's not what I've heard."

"Heard from whom?"

Millie ignored the question. "Tell me *exactly* what's been going on here."

After the day she'd had, Julie simply didn't have the energy to spar with Millie. So she sighed. "Can I possibly sit down to tell it? It's lengthy."

Millie nodded. "In the library."

They walked back to the dark paneled room that held the smell of old books—a combination of dry leather, ancient ink, and mustiness. As they settled down, Inga stepped into the doorway.

"May I bring you coffee and pastry?" Inga directed her question at Millie.

Millie smiled brightly back. "You're a love as always. Yes, please, bring us a tray."

Inga nodded and backed out. Julie quietly began to fill Millie in on everything that had happened from the moment Daniel walked into the inn. She left out anything tied to her own colorful past and skirted around possible illegal activity on her part, but beyond that, she gave an honest account of the events.

In the middle of the spiel, she paused when Inga brought in the tray. Millie thanked her and the dour-faced woman left. Julie sighed. "I wish I knew why Inga disliked me so."

Millie shook her head, making her iron-gray curls bounce. "I doubt it's you. Inga's a lamb, but she doesn't like change."

Julie couldn't imagine Inga as a "lamb" or a "love," but she decided she was close enough to being fired without insulting someone Millie clearly liked. She wrapped up her recital of events with the trip into the cornfield, then sat back and waited to be fired.

Millie's eyes widened. "What a horrible experience. Are you all right?"

"I'm fine. I was shaky for a while, but the farmer and his wife were really nice."

Millie looked her over, her eyes sharp. Finally she said, "I don't like the fact that someone is willing to be so violent over this." She paused. "But it's undoubtedly the most excitement Straussberg has seen in decades. No wonder the guests are so thrilled."

"Thrilled?" Julie scoffed. "They demanded I throw Daniel out on the street."

"Yes, I heard that too. But the whispers I've caught since I got home have mostly been full of excitement at the mystery of it. I suspect the people pretending to worry about blood-thirsty killers are secretly delighted to be so close to a murder mystery. It's a big adventure."

"It's hard for me to see it that way," Julie said. "I knew George and liked him. He was sweet and funny."

Millie's bright expression turned sad. "I am sorry about that. I never met him, of course, nor did any of the guests. I imagine it's like a television drama for them."

"I suppose."

Millie seemed to turn that over in her head for a few moments. Then her face brightened again. "Maybe we could figure out some way to bring guests that sense of adventure without so much misfortune. We should consider having mystery weekends at the inn."

"It would certainly be different," Julie said.

"We'll have to decide when to have our first one. Halloween would be marvelous, but that doesn't leave us enough time to plan a special event like that."

That reference reminded Julie of the one event she'd failed to include in her recitation. "We may have another function to schedule." She told Millie about Mrs. Parson's interest in having a fundraiser for the senator at the inn because of her fond memories of the place.

Millie's brows knit together while she tried to call up memories of so long ago. "I don't really remember them, but that doesn't mean much. That far back, I'd only remember people who made trouble, and it sounds like they wouldn't have."

"No, Mrs. Parson seemed very gracious," Julie said.

Inga bustled in to collect the tray, commenting as she did so, "Mrs. Parson is an angel and so is her husband."

"You know her?" Millie asked.

"Of course not," Inga said, her slight German accent making her sound stern. "I'd not be knowing a senator or his wife. But I do know that my brother would have lost his farm if not for Senator Parson. Michael's wife wrote to the senator about the situation, and the man personally got involved and helped. The senator didn't have to do such a thing, but he did."

"That's lovely," Millie said. "Well, I'll have to call Mrs. Parson and check on her final decision about the venue. It would be a lot of work to get ready for an event like that, but I'd love to meet an angel or two."

"You're making fun of me," Inga said stiffly.

Millie smiled, a twinkle in her eye. "Only now and then."

Julie spent another hour or so going over figures and plans with Millie and listening to the woman's stories of her whirlwind tour of popular Missouri tourist traps.

"This was only the first step," Millie said. "When I leave again, I plan to spend two full weeks in Branson, then I'm going to Tennessee."

Julie smiled at the way Millie said "Tennessee" as if it were a distant land. "I'm glad you won't need a passport."

"Sure, you laugh at my trips," Millie said. "But you try being plunked in one place for nearly your whole life. You'd take baby steps too."

Julie didn't think that she would. She wasn't really the baby-steps type in anything she did. It was one of the things that drove her dear friend Hannah crazy. Which reminded

Julie that when she finished up for the day, Hannah would definitely want an update.

And she did.

"Senator North sounds disgusting," Hannah said when Julie finished filling her in. "But my money is on the lawyer as the genius behind the road-rage incident. I doubt it's a coincidence that you ended up in a cornfield shortly after finishing your conversation with him."

"He does seem like the type who wouldn't mind being violent," Julie said as she picked at the salad her friend had made her for supper. "But I think it's suspicious that Senator Parson knew who I was."

Hannah shrugged. "Of course, it might have been something simple, like his wife was visiting, saw you outside, and mentioned it to her husband, who then realized you weren't likely to be both an innkeeper and a magazine reporter."

"So another coincidence. They're piling up a bit around the senator."

"True, but the lawyer sounds more like the sort of creep who'd run you off the road. I can practically picture him doing it."

Julie huffed, absently stabbing at a piece of lettuce. "I just wish I'd actually met Senator Parson. I would like to get some kind of reading on the man. See how genuine he seems."

"He'd hardly be likely to spill any dastardly deeds while you talked to him."

"No, but right now he's nothing but a big blank hole in all of this. Is he the angel that Inga believes him to be? Or is he a monster who killed Daniel's best friend?"

Hannah frowned at Julie's salad. "Either eat that salad or bury it. You've stabbed it enough. You know, it would be helpful if you had some kind of motive for any of these people."

Julie shoved a bit of salad into her mouth and nodded. "That is an issue. None of them seem to be tied to Daniel or to Winkler Farm. The closest would probably be Parson, but that's because he likes to help out farmers, which doesn't exactly make him a villain."

"The lawyer," Hannah said. "We know he tried to buy Winkler Farm to stop the excavation."

"On behalf of someone else."

"So he claims. Not everything a guy like him says is necessarily true."

Julie accepted that. She could imagine Randall Cantor cheerfully lying right to her face. "But *why* would he want it?"

"That's the million-dollar question. When you try and answer it, please, do so without any breaking and entering."

Julie shrugged. "I already broke and entered, and I didn't learn anything useful. I need another way."

As Julie walked through the inn, checking locks and reassuring herself that her work for the day was done, she wondered how she might learn more about Cantor. The contractor who was dating the lawyer's mother would probably be happy to talk about him, but considering the bad feelings between them, Julie doubted the man was Cantor's confidant. She wondered if it would be worthwhile to pay another visit to the lawyer's uncle. He might know some family stories.

She still wasn't settled on a plan of action when she climbed the stairs to the third floor. She put the kettle on and rummaged through her packets of herbal tea until she found chamomile. She needed all the help she could get in relaxing for sleep after the day she'd been through. Her muscles were beginning to ache from the accident.

She was in the middle of debating whether it was worthwhile to hunt for her bottle of aspirin when her phone rang.

She groaned as she shifted to pull the phone out of her blazer pocket. The note from the senator came out with the phone. Julie frowned at it before tossing it onto the table beside her.

"Julie!" Daniel half-shouted in her ear. "It's been a fantastic day."

"It has?"

"We found a boot. It's perfectly preserved. I couldn't believe it. You would expect the mud to be so wet that things degrade, but this boot looked like it was lost yesterday."

"It must be an exciting boot."

"It is, but more than that, it means we're beginning to dig up cargo. At the speed we're working, we'll be uncovering crates within the next few days. Once we bring up the first crock or crate, I'm going to work this site around the clock."

"Your crew will be thrilled."

"When I pay them all that overtime, I'm sure they will. You should come out and see the site soon. It's nothing like the big hole you saw last. With the earthmoving machines, we've got it looking more like a small, very muddy valley."

"Sounds enchanting."

He chuckled. "Beauty is in the eye of the beholder, I suppose. Still, once we start bringing up containers, we're bound to discover a link to that message you decoded."

Julie's attention sharpened. She'd nearly forgotten the coded message for the treasure. She was trying to call it up in her tired thoughts when Daniel simply recited it from memory. "'Mey apples fill the finest crock and hew a space for Southern stock.' As soon as I haul up the first crock, I'll call you. You can be here when we unseal the thing."

"You expect the crocks to be sealed?"

She could almost hear his shrug. "It was common, especially with perishable goods. The crock would be sealed with wax to make it airtight and slow decay. Of course, after all this time, I doubt any contents will be fresh, even in the cold mud."

"Do you expect to find apples?" she asked, then she remembered. "'Mey apples.' Is that a kind of apple?"

"A mayapple is actually a kind of wildflower that you can find in the woods," Daniel said. "But the spelling is different. Of course, inventive spelling isn't all that unusual from that time. Even a ship's captain might not be the best of spellers."

"Maybe," Julie said. "But what if 'Mey' is a clue to the identity of the owner of the treasure?"

"That would make sense."

She sighed. "Too bad none of our suspects has 'Mey' in their names."

"Not today, but who knows what a good genealogist could shake out of their family trees? I have a friend I could call. ..."

Julie laughed. "You seem to have a friend to call in all situations."

"What can I say? I'm a friendly guy. Anyway, she's also a historian. Her specialty is genealogical research. I can give her our list of suspects and set her on the trail in search of Meys."

"Since I'm mostly out of leads, that wouldn't hurt," Julie said gloomily. "I should tell you about *my* day. It hasn't gone quite as swimmingly as yours." She began at the beginning, telling him of her drive to Jefferson City.

"You went investigating without me?"

"You were so excited to get back to the dig. I hated to pull you away."

"That's true enough. I forgive you. Hold on a sec," he said. Julie heard the sound of Daniel moving around in the bunkhouse. Finally he came back on the line. "Julie, I'm going to need to ring you back. I hear something moving around outside, and I want to check on the site. I can't afford any vandalism now with us so close to bringing up real cargo."

"No!" Julie exclaimed. "Do *not* go out there alone." She growled as she realized she was shouting at the dial tone. Staring at her phone, she wondered if she should call the police. Daniel wouldn't be happy if they arrived in time to find he'd heard a deer or a raccoon savaging around the bunkhouse. Still, she couldn't sit around and wait to see if he called back.

She shoved her feet into her shoes and ran all the way down to the first floor. She barely remembered to lock up behind her before dashing to the car. The drive out to Winkler Farm seemed to take forever, though Julie had certainly pushed the car well past the speed limit for most of it.

She took the turn into the farm at enough speed to make the car complain as it bounced and rumbled over the dirt road. She was just around the bend from the farm stand when she saw flames. One of the outbuildings was on fire, and Julie had a sick suspicion she knew which one.

Someone set the bunkhouse on fire. Julie raced ahead with her heart in her throat, praying Daniel wasn't trapped inside the burning building.

EIGHTEEN

Julie drove as close as she dared to the old bunkhouse, then steered the car off the dirt road so fire trucks could get by. She had the car door open as soon as she jerked the key from the ignition. "Daniel!"

She ran for the bunkhouse and could feel the heat on her face when a voice yelled, "Julie!"

She turned away from the fire and blinked her light-dazzled eyes. She could make out two dark shapes leaning against a small tractor. "Daniel?"

"It's Joseph Winkler. Daniel's over here."

Julie crossed the distance in seconds, careless of the uneven ground. She found Daniel sitting on the edge of some large, mysterious piece of farm equipment. He was bent at the waist with his hands on his knees, head down. His breathing was raspy with an occasional cough. "Are you all right?" she asked.

He nodded. "Thanks to Joe."

Julie turned to look at Joe Winkler. "I was taking a walk," he said. "I smelled smoke and followed the scent to the bunkhouse. Someone had shoved a chisel into the crack between the door and the frame to wedge it shut, then dragged a bale of hay into the plantings under one of the windows and set it on fire."

She turned back to Daniel. "Someone was trying to kill you."

He coughed. "So it would appear. If Joe hadn't gotten the door open when he did, the smoke would have killed me long before the fire. The window was cracked where the fire was set, and I couldn't close it. Someone had nailed it partly open.

And I couldn't open any of the others for the same reason."

"On the phone, I thought you were going outside to check on a noise."

"I was. I did. I barely got out the front door before someone clunked me on the head in the dark. I wasn't knocked out, but I wasn't in any shape to fight back when the guy shoved me back through the front door."

"Someone put a lot of effort into this," Julie said, then turned back to Joseph. "You didn't see anyone?"

The farmer shook his head. "No, but I wasn't looking either. The fire had my attention, and getting Daniel out. I put out the fire with the garden hose, but I also called 911. They should be here soon. They know the way."

He'd barely finished speaking before they heard sirens. Things became very chaotic after that as people swarmed around the bunkhouse and around Daniel.

Julie spotted Detective Frost in the mix and walked over to him. "I thought I'd come over and hear how you think Daniel managed to knock himself in the head and then trap himself inside the bunkhouse," she said.

Detective Frost gave her a look as chilly as his name. "I'm always open to revising a theory with new evidence. I admit it's unlikely your boyfriend did this, though it would be a great way to throw us off the trail."

"Wow." Julie blinked. "That was the least definitive admission of a mistake that I've ever heard."

The detective tilted his head to one side. "Speaking of hearing things, I understand you've been harassing people in town."

"I have not. ..."

He held up a hand to stop her. "The complaint came from someone with a history of stretching the truth. That's why you haven't heard from me about it."

Julie assumed that meant the source was the lawyer. If anyone would know what a scumbag the man was, it would be a cop.

"My greater concern is this amateur investigating you seem to be doing," Detective Frost said. "That kind of thing can get you hurt."

"I'm well aware of that." Julie went on to describe the SUV running her off the road.

"Why didn't you tell me about this before now?" Frost demanded.

Over the detective's shoulder, Julie saw that Daniel had gotten free of the ambulance techs and was walking toward her, a bit more unsteadily than she'd like. His face was dark with sooty grime and concern.

"There was nothing to tell. My car didn't sustain serious damage, though the cornfield I drove through is definitely the worse for wear." She turned back to the detective. "But I'm obviously rattling some cages."

"Miss Ellis, you're putting yourself in danger needlessly," Detective Frost said. "I can handle the investigation fine without the help of Nancy Drew."

"Aren't you interested in what I've turned up?" she asked. "I have several suspects, including two state senators. And since someone ran me off the road today, I'm inclined to think one of the people I'm investigating is the killer."

"State senators?" Detective Frost shook his head. "You can't go around accusing state senators of murder when there is absolutely no evidence to back it up."

"They're both clients of your unreliable accuser!" Julie exclaimed, her patience wearing thin.

"Bad taste in lawyers isn't illegal."

"Please, could we not yell?" Daniel asked in his raspy rumble. "My head is killing me. Julie, I'm afraid I'm beginning to agree with Detective Frost. George is dead, I nearly died tonight, and you could have been killed this afternoon. We need to let the police handle this."

"And if you continue with this," the detective added, "I won't be able to protect you from the legal action that's sure to come from you harassing people."

"I don't need you to protect me," Julie snapped. "I'm fully capable of protecting myself."

With an exasperated sigh, the detective turned and walked off toward the men poking around the bunkhouse.

Julie switched her focus to Daniel. "Shouldn't you be on your way to the hospital?"

"Now you sound like the techs," he said. "I'm fine." At that, he swayed slightly and Julie quickly stepped closer to support him.

"You're clearly not a good judge of your own condition. You can ride to the hospital in the ambulance or I can drive you. You pick."

He frowned at her but didn't argue. "I'll take the ambulance. Sitting in the waiting area of the emergency room is never much fun."

"Fine. I'll follow in my car."

Julie handed him off to the ambulance techs and watched as they pulled out. Then she headed for her car. Joseph Winkler caught her before she could climb in. "Are you on the way to the hospital?"

"Yes."

"Tell Daniel that I'll get the bunkhouse aired out, but he probably can't stay in it for a day or two. I could put him in our guest room up at the house if he needs a place in the meantime."

"I don't know if he'll want to bring his troubles right into your house," she said. "I'll probably take him back to the inn with me."

"I thought the guests were scared of him."

"What they don't know won't scare them," Julie said. "I'll put him in my room if I have to." She thanked Joseph again for everything and hopped into her car.

At the hospital, Julie managed to slip into the emergency area to wait with Daniel. She stood beside his gurney in one of the curtained-off emergency room bays and listened while he complained that he really was fine.

After X-rays were taken, the doctor confirmed that Daniel had a mild concussion. "I think he'll be fine," she told Julie. "But we'd like to keep him for the rest of the night for observation."

Daniel immediately climbed off the gurney to stand, swaying beside it. "Forget that. I've had enough hospital."

The doctor hurried over to block his exit. "Sit down before you fall down."

"He can be stubborn," Julie warned.

Daniel sat down next to the gurney in the chair Julie had dragged in. "I'm not staying."

The doctor regarded him for a moment. "I could release him *if* he has someone who will stay with him through the night. He can't be alone, and he needs to take it easy for a couple of days."

"I'll take him back to stay with me," Julie said. "I can keep an eye on him. I shouldn't let him sleep, right?"

The doctor smiled. "He can sleep. With children, we suggest parents rouse them every few hours just to be certain they can be awakened, but as long as he isn't showing other symptoms, sleep will be good for him."

The doctor filled her in on symptoms to watch for and scolded Daniel a little more before she finally let them go. Daniel grumbled about not being an invalid as an attendant rolled him out to Julie's car in a wheelchair.

When they reached the inn, the sun was barely clearing the horizon. Julie stayed close to Daniel as he shuffled up the steps. She unlocked the front door and held it open. "You can have my bed," she whispered. "I'll sleep on the sofa."

"That doesn't sound fair," he said at his normal volume, and Julie winced as the sound seemed to rumble around the entryway.

"Stealth really isn't your gift, is it?" she muttered, slipping under Daniel's arm when he bumped into the wall. Between the concussion and the sleepless night, she wondered how well he'd manage to climb all the stairs to the third floor.

Julie guided him toward the main stairway.

"You must have had some night."

Julie spun to face Millie, who smiled cheerfully at her.

"This isn't the way it looks," Julie said.

Millie's brows rose. "So you aren't sneaking a man up to your room?"

"I'm an adult," Julie said. "I don't sneak men to my room."

Millie looked Daniel over from the top of his head to his feet. "Your friend looks like he's had a rough night."

"I was knocked on the head and locked in a building to burn to death. So all in all, I'm doing great." Daniel managed a smile and held out his hand. "Daniel Franklin. Pleased to meet you."

Julie groaned. She hadn't intended to admit she was bringing *Daniel* back.

"I look forward to hearing more about that." Millie gave Julie a pointed look, then turned back to Daniel with a smile.

"I've heard a lot about your hunt for the steamship. Are you wanting a room? Something tells me you don't know much about quilting."

"I'd do my quilt block trick and prove you wrong," Daniel said. "But my head hurts."

"Quilt block trick? You'll have to show me when you're feeling better." She turned back to Julie. "He can have the third-floor room again—if he promises not to get into any trouble."

Julie raised her eyebrows. "Really? Aren't you worried about how the guests will react?"

"Oh please, I've never seen such a tittering bunch of quilters. They love all this drama and mystery. I may advertise him as an amenity."

"I really appreciate this," Daniel said.

"You best get your friend upstairs," Millie said to Julie. "And maybe grab a couple of hours of sleep yourself. I can hold down the fort this morning. Then we can chat some this afternoon."

"Thanks."

Though they were far from quick, Julie finally managed to get Daniel up to his tower room.

"Wasn't I supposed to do something today?" Daniel asked as he tentatively touched the back of his head. "I seem to remember we talked about me contacting someone today."

"A genealogist," Julie said. "To track down any connections between our suspects and the name 'Mey.'"

"Right," he said. "I remember that now. My friend is a historian in North Carolina. I'll give her a call and put her on the job. She's obsessed with the pre–Civil War South. She might already have some material on the family if they were well-to-do."

"That sounds like a good next step. But first, you need to get to bed. You don't look like you're in any shape to make phone calls."

He smiled. "You sure know how to punch a guy in the ego."

"You'll survive."

Julie guided Daniel over to the bed. She helped him remove his heavy boots. He left the rest of his clothes on and was asleep in minutes. Julie pulled the chair closer to the bed and sat down. She'd promised not to leave Daniel alone, and she intended to keep that promise. She leaned forward and rested her forearms on the bed, intending to rest her head for a moment. In seconds, she was deeply asleep.

Daniel woke Julie several hours later and announced he was feeling considerably better. He asked if there was any chance he could get something to eat. Considering that Daniel was the one who'd had the worse night, Julie didn't have the heart to beg for another hour to sleep. "I'll go down to the kitchen and see what I can find."

She was shocked to find the kitchen bustling. Mrs. Parson and Millie sat at the antique trestle table next to the windows that looked out across the backyard. The senator's wife greeted Julie with a warm smile. "I'm glad to see you again. I was just telling Millie that you were a wonderful representative of the inn on my last visit."

"Does your return mean we'll be hosting the fundraiser?" Julie asked.

The stylish woman's smile turned rueful. "I'm sorry to say that Walter's campaign manager felt the inn wasn't upscale enough." She turned to look at Millie. "That man wouldn't know a charming venue if it bit him on the nose. I reminded Walter that this place was perfect, cozy, and warm, but I was outvoted."

"I suppose that's the American way," Millie said.

"True." Mrs. Parson sighed. "I do miss the days when we didn't put so much time into campaigning and fundraising, when we were more of a couple and less of a political machine."

"It was awfully nice of you to drive all the way to the inn to say we weren't getting the job," Julie said.

Mrs. Parson looked at Julie and chuckled. "I'm not that nice. I had to be in the area anyway on campaign business, and I couldn't resist. I have so many fond memories of the inn. Plus, my visit before inspired me to get back into quilting. I can't let my whole life be defined by politics. Millie is helping me choose a project that will be portable and simple enough for someone like me who's very rusty."

It was only then that Julie noticed the handful of patterns on the table, scattered among the tea things.

"I know you'll find something perfect," Julie said. "If you won't think me terribly rude, I was going to fix myself something to eat."

"Please," Mrs. Parson said. "You certainly won't bother us."

Julie walked back to the counter beside Hannah, who opened the fridge and pulled out a lunch bag. "I fixed sandwiches for you and Daniel," she whispered. "Millie told me about last night since *you* didn't."

"Thanks," Julie said. "You're a saint." She took one more look over at the senator's wife and Millie, sitting with their heads together and chatting like old friends.

Following her gaze, Hannah whispered, "I know what you're thinking. But Mrs. Parson doesn't exactly ooze criminal mastermind."

Julie sighed. That was true. But what about her husband?

Nineteen

Daniel was back at the excavation and staying at the Winklers' bunkhouse again within two days. His team immediately began unearthing cargo. With Millie at the inn, Julie didn't dare sneak out to the excavation site, but she could practically feel a magnetic pull in that direction every day. Finally, by the third day, Millie snagged her by the arm and drew her into the library.

"I've decided to stick around for the next few weeks," Millie announced. "I have to admit, I'm eager to see what Daniel finds. That said, I've decided you should be our eyes and ears in the field."

"Which means?" Julie asked.

"You can go to the excavation site every morning after breakfast is squared away and any planned guest outings have begun. I always appreciate your help for those. After that, I can handle things here, and you can drive out to the site."

Julie practically danced in place, finally giving in to the urge to hug Millie. "Thank you! After everything that's happened, it's hard to wait around for reports that don't come until late in the day."

"I do have one stipulation."

"Yes?"

"When you get back here—at a reasonable hour each evening—you must have a little impromptu 'treasure hunt tales' session in the dining room for our guests. They're so fired up about all this, and I know they'd find it exciting."

"Oh, I'm not much of a storyteller," Julie said. "That's really Shirley's gift."

A cheerful voice practically shouted from the doorway. "Maybe she could write up notes, and I could tell the story for her!"

Millie turned to the doorway and crossed her arms. "Didn't your mama ever tell you not to eavesdrop, Shirley Estelle Ott?"

Shirley's voice was completely unrepentant as she stepped into the room. "But I would miss out on so much!"

"Storytelling *is* Shirley's thing," Julie said.

"But you're the one going out to the site," Millie said. "Unless you think I should send Shirley out there while you watch the tea-and-quilt shop …?"

"Sure!" Shirley chirped.

"Nope," Julie said. "I'll be happy to do the talks."

"Oh, fine," Shirley said, obviously disappointed. "I should go find Inga and see if you've given away any of her jobs lately!" She sashayed out, making the silky strips of her gypsy-inspired skirt swish.

Julie turned back to Millie. "I hate that she's miffed at me."

"She'll get over it. Now, you had a list of possible repairs and replacements you wanted to go over? We should do that before you dash off to hunt for treasure."

Later, at the excavation site, Julie was amazed at all the activity. Daniel had added a swarm of new people. He introduced her around quickly, but she doubted she could remember half the names and almost none of their various specialties. Clearly Daniel had a lot of friends in academia.

While she watched, the team pulled a metal-bound trunk from the mud and opened it. Julie was astounded by the contents: wool jackets and pants that looked nearly ready to put on.

She reached out and touched one of the jackets. Though it was worn, she marveled at how perfectly intact it looked and felt. The wool was a lovely shade of smoky blue. All the edges were trimmed in a neat braid of the same color, and the large buttons were covered in the same blue wool. The hand-stitched buttonholes were flawless. The garment had turned-back cuffs and looked as if it were tailor-made for a specific person with the many gussets shaping the jacket. She wished she could take it to show the quilters. She knew they would appreciate the workmanship on the piece.

"Leave it to a quilter to appreciate the clothes," Daniel said, watching her with a smile.

Julie smiled back, though she wasn't sure she deserved to be called a quilter. She made a promise to herself to start a project the second all the treasure hunting and mystery was over.

After the trunk, they hauled up a barrel. When they broke the seal, Julie peeked inside, her head right beside Daniel's. The barrel was full of white china dishes adorned with a delicate blue edge trim. Even the excelsior packing material was still preserved.

At the end of the day, Julie found her "treasure hunt" talk at the inn was easy. She simply described what she'd seen and touched. The quilters listened avidly as they stitched away on their projects, and all of them had questions, especially about the clothing pieces. They talked about trims and designs.

"One of the last things Daniel unearthed today was a trunk full of roughly made red shirts with crude hearts stitched on them," Julie said. "These shirts were lighter fabric and not as well preserved, but it was interesting to see these hearts with braid trim around them."

"Those designs were political," Shirley interjected from her spot in the doorway. All eyes turned to her. "Men in the border territories wore designs that showed how they felt about slavery before the war."

"What did the heart signify?" one of the quilters asked.

Shirley lit up like a firefly. She breezed into the room and took her place beside Julie. "It was a pro-slavery symbol."

The woman who'd asked the question wrinkled her nose, and Shirley went on, her voice taking on a storyteller tone. "Just imagine the sort of man those shirts were heading for. He'd wear a pair of long boots with a rifle swung over his shoulder and a sword by his side. Maybe a wicked Bowie knife sticking out of one of the boots, and a pair of revolvers thrust into a leather belt."

"That's a lot of weapons," a wide-eyed young woman said as she held her needle frozen over her quilting hoop.

"Those were rough times. And a man had to know where another man stood on the issue of slavery. So they'd wear a mark right on their shirts, and braid was almost always used in the design. A heart, an anchor, an eagle—they all meant something."

Julie looked at Shirley in admiration. "You've done a lot of research."

"That's how I make *my* Stories and Stitches so memorable," Shirley said proudly. She took over for the rest of the talk, and the quilters around the table seemed to like that just fine.

Shirley joined in on the treasure hunt stories every night after that. Julie would describe what she'd seen, and Shirley would interpret it. They made a good team. The room was always packed. Julie noticed that Inga made an appearance every night as well, though she usually lurked in the doorway with her face tightly pinched in disapproval.

Everything seemed to be going well, which made Julie nervous. In her experience, life was never calm for long. Plus, anyone willing to set fires and even kill would hardly give up without a fight. If the attacks really were linked to the shipwreck, she couldn't imagine that the killer would lose interest now that Daniel was bringing up the ship's contents.

At the end of the week, Julie got an extra surprise when she drove out to the site. Daniel stood talking to the most beautiful woman she had ever seen. Like Julie, the woman was tall and slender with long dark hair. But where Julie's hair was a mass of curls that always seemed on the edge of springing out of control, the woman beside Daniel looked sleek and flawless.

Julie fought the urge to hate her on sight. She walked up to them with a painful smile.

Daniel spotted her and waved. "Julie, my friend Louisa has found some fascinating information."

"Louisa?"

The woman offered Julie a cool hand. "Louisa Sharp. I've been doing genealogical research for Danny."

Julie turned and mouthed, "Danny?"

Daniel's face reddened. "Louisa discovered a family name tied to the ship: Meyhew."

The revelation pulled Julie's attention away from the other woman's clothes and poise. "Meyhew ... like 'Mey apples'?"

"Just the same," Daniel said. "But I should let Louisa tell it."

The smile Louisa gave Daniel looked anything but professional, distracting Julie again. Then the woman spoke in her light Southern drawl. "The Meyhew family owned a very successful plantation in Mississippi. Unfortunately, Elizabeth Meyhew, the wife, ran off with a mysterious stranger and took along most of the Meyhews' portable wealth. Gold, small sculptures, and an extensive collection of extremely valuable jewelry went missing along with the wife. The only unexpected thing she left behind was a young son, Nathaniel."

Daniel cut in then, his voice excited. "Louisa told me that some people didn't believe Meyhews' tale. They thought Elizabeth was carrying the valuables North to one of the unaligned territories so they wouldn't have to contribute to the Confederate cause, and that the story was simply a front for that."

"In that case, wouldn't the wife have returned eventually?" Julie asked.

"If she did, there is no record of it," Louisa said. "She vanished completely. Much like *The Grand Adventure*."

"So are either of our senators or the lawyer related to the Meyhews?" Julie asked.

Louisa shook her head. "Not that I can find. Laurence Meyhew never remarried after his wife left. I did find a fairly lurid book that contains some information that may interest you about the Meyhews." She opened the leather tote she carried and pulled out an old book, handing it over to Julie. "I imagine you have more time to read it, puttering around an inn as you do."

Julie ignored the dig and turned the book over in her hand. The cloth covering of the binding was worn. She flipped it open and saw it had been published in 1925. The title, *Southern Secrets*, was not encouraging about its authenticity.

"I looked into some information on that author," Louisa said. "In case your connection might be along that genealogical line. This man is virtually the only one to have written extensively about the Meyhew scandal. Apparently the author was a bit unstable. He killed himself when he finished writing it. The manuscript was published five years later by his only son. Not long after that, the son died as well, from a heart attack. Since he was unmarried, the line stopped with him. So I suppose you might say the book is cursed."

Julie thought Shirley would probably say exactly that about it. She leafed through the pages.

"Only a few copies of that exist," Louisa added. "It was tricky to find."

"I appreciate your effort on this," Daniel said. "I owe you one."

The smile Louisa gave him in return was more than friendly. Julie was surprised at the pang of jealousy she felt. It's wasn't like she and Daniel were involved. They were just ... good friends.

Even so, she sort of hoped the perfect Louisa fell into the Missouri mud before the end of the day.

Julie cleared her throat, drawing their attention back to her. "You tracked down the whole Meyhew line?"

"It wasn't a particularly complicated one," Louisa said. "Laurence had a son, Nathaniel, who had a son, William. William then had a son, Jackson. Apparently, male babies ran in the family. I haven't been able to find out what happened to Jackson. Technically, he might still be alive, though elderly. He apparently left Mississippi, but I haven't tracked him down. I have, however, traced the family tree of both your senators and the lawyer. Jackson Meyhew is not lurking in it."

Julie felt a wash of disappointment. She'd really hoped there was a clear link tying one of her suspects to the shipwreck itself.

"It was a long shot anyway," Daniel said, his voice reflecting Julie's gloom. "I can't imagine why anyone today would care about such an old scandal anyway."

Louisa smiled as they walked closer to the excavation. "On the bright side, if Mrs. Meyhew did come aboard *The Grand Adventure* with the family jewels, you might have some interesting things yet to discover down in that mud pit."

TWENTY

To Julie's enormous relief, the gorgeous genealogist couldn't stay long.

"I have to leave in the morning to get back," Louisa said with a pout. "I have classes to teach at the university on Monday."

"An academic's life is always busy," Daniel replied cheerfully.

Louisa obviously didn't share any interest in the muddy artifacts that excited Daniel so much, though she did talk him into a dinner date.

"That would be great," Daniel said. "We can talk more about the history of the wreck. I'd like to show you what I have on the ship's captain." He glanced toward Julie. "You might find this interesting as well. Do you want to have dinner with us?"

Louisa looked at Daniel with irritation. "I'm sure Miss Ellis is far too busy with her innkeeping."

"Actually, Millie has encouraged my involvement in the excavation. She'd love it if I learned more about the captain for the nightly treasure talks I've been giving."

Daniel clapped his hands. "Fantastic! That's set then."

Julie didn't know if Daniel's obliviousness was more endearing or frustrating, but she liked the scowl that marred Louisa's pretty face.

One of the men in the excavation pit yelled up, "I've found a crock!"

"Excellent!" Daniel raced toward the pit, and the two women trailed him. "I've been looking forward to the first crock. The contents will be airtight, so we could see the best preservation of artifacts so far."

A mud-caked workman handed the big crock to Daniel. From where Julie stood, it looked as much like a giant wad of mud as a crock. Daniel carried it carefully out of the excavation ditch and scraped the mud from the ceramic. It ended up being a little bigger than a traditional butter churn. Julie gasped when she saw a dull blue mayapple wildflower stenciled on the side of the crock.

Daniel carefully broke the seal on the crock. He reached into the crock and pulled out a small leather bag. He looked up at Julie, his eyes full of wonder. "The leather is still supple."

He opened the bag and poured gold coins into Julie's hand. The metal was cold against her skin, and the coins shone in the autumn sun. Daniel picked up a coin and turned it over. "These are Spanish."

"Amazing," Louisa said, her voice a little breathy. She had crept a bit closer, though she eyed the muddy ground with distaste. "Are there more bags of coins in there?"

Daniel handed Julie the leather pouch, and she carefully put the coins back in. He turned back to the crock and thrust his hand in. "There's a bottom, but it is set way too high." He pulled his knife out of the sheath and carefully wedged out the false bottom made from wax. With the false bottom out, he stuck his hand back in.

He pulled out a skull.

Louisa shrieked, backing away so rapidly that her stylish shoes slipped in the mud and she fell, sliding down the muddy bank until she was halfway to the bottom of the excavation trench. Several workmen rushed to help her back out.

Meanwhile, Julie and Daniel remained riveted on the

skull. "The Meyhew treasure isn't quite what I expected," she said, studying the vacant holes.

Daniel turned the skull over carefully. "Someone flayed all the flesh off this before putting it in the crock."

Julie winced. "Maybe it's some kind of ancient artifact?"

He shook his head slowly. "If it is, the person didn't die so nicely." He turned the skull over to show the backside where a spiderweb of cracks made it clear the original owner of the skull had been struck in the head—hard.

The crock contained more bones—lots more bones—but not enough to make up a full skeleton. Since any finding of human remains technically had to be reported, Daniel called the police. While they waited, the team unearthed two more crocks. Each held valuables and bones.

All excavation stopped as soon as the police arrived. Once again, Daniel's excavation became a potential crime scene. "I won't close the scene long if these really are old," Detective Frost said. "But I'm going to have an officer here for the rest of your excavation. If you turn up any more dead people, I want to have someone on site."

Julie called the inn to tell Millie she'd need to postpone her treasure talk for a night. She explained about the discovery of the skull. "At least this murder wasn't someone you know," Millie said sympathetically.

"I'm going to have supper with Daniel, and we'll wait to hear what the coroner has to say about the bones."

"That'll be fine," Millie said. "I'm going to have to start taking reservations for your talks. I'm not sure we're going to have a room big enough to fit everyone who will want to come. I could put you in the breakfast room, but do we really want murder associated with that room?"

"Probably not," Julie said, feeling a little overwhelmed.

Louisa returned to her hotel room to change as soon as the police said she could go. She reminded Daniel about their dinner plans. "We could meet in the hotel restaurant," she said sweetly. "It seems nice."

"That will be fine. Julie and I will meet you there."

Louisa gave Julie the stink eye, then stalked across the mud to her car. Hours later, Julie and Daniel were ready to call it a day. Daniel looked down at his dirty clothes. "How fancy is the hotel restaurant?"

"I don't know," Julie answered.

"I'm afraid if I stop to change, I'll collapse. We should just go."

"Sounds good." Julie smiled, certain Louisa would be less than thrilled that Daniel didn't dress up for her.

They'd barely sat down in the restaurant before Daniel got the call from Detective Frost. He said "yes" and "uh-huh" several times before hanging up. Then he announced, "The excavation can resume the day after tomorrow. The coroner placed time of death at over a hundred and fifty years ago, so the excavation can't exactly be considered a crime scene. Also, the coroner said the bones belonged to a woman."

"So you may have found Meyhew's runaway wife," Julie said. "What kind of man kills his wife, flays off her flesh, and ships her bones away with the family jewels?"

Louisa sipped her glass of water, eyeing Julie sharply over the edge. "It would certainly explain why no one ever saw the woman again."

Julie sighed. "We get more and more information, but none of it connects. Even if Laurence Meyhew shipped his dead wife along with the family treasure, there's still no link to any of our suspects."

Louisa shrugged. "Maybe you haven't looked at the right suspects."

That's a depressing thought. If none of their suspects was the killer, Julie had no idea where to turn next—and no idea why anyone would have threatened her, threatened Hannah, killed George, and tried to kill Daniel. The whole thing made her head ache.

The rest of dinner consisted of good food and lots of tension. Louisa took veiled digs at Julie at every opportunity. Daniel seemed oblivious as he rattled on about the dig. On the positive side, Julie went home certain that Daniel had no real interest in Louisa. The *only* thing he seemed interested in was the excavation.

"I've been thrown over for a mud hole," she muttered as she drove back to the inn, but then she reminded herself that she didn't want the complication of a romance anyway. And she'd gone to great lengths to make that clear to Daniel.

The next day at the inn passed in a blur. A large group finished their stay, and a small one checked in, bringing with them dozens of questions about area attractions. Julie suspected they wouldn't be doing much quilting as the list of things they wanted to see grew. With so much coming and going back-to-back, Julie offered to help Inga make up rooms.

The housekeeper stood at rigid attention when Julie made the offer. "Is my work inadequate?" Inga asked stiffly.

"No, of course not. But we're in a crunch to get the new group into rooms."

Inga seemed to shudder as she considered this, but she nodded curtly. "You may remove the used bedding and carry it down to the laundry room. I will make up the beds with the fresh."

Julie almost saluted but decided the older woman wouldn't

appreciate the snarky gesture. She headed into the first room and began removing the bed linens. From the corner of her eye, she caught movement out in the hall, but the doorway was empty when she turned to look.

Stripping the beds didn't take long. Julie bundled in the used towels and hauled all the dirty linens down the back stairwell to the laundry room. Unlike the beautiful kitchen, the laundry room was in need of a fresh coat of paint and a new floor. Still, the chipped tile was clean, and the appliances sparkled. Apparently Inga didn't believe in letting dirt touch any area where she went regularly.

After Julie got the two washers loaded, she decided not to offer Inga any more help. Clearly, sharing her domain was stressful for the housekeeper. Julie cut through the kitchen to head back to the front desk. She found Millie and Hannah discussing food.

Millie beamed at Julie. "Your talk tonight will be in the breakfast room. I simply cannot fit all the people in the dining room. And since we're using the breakfast room, we're going to offer snacks and drinks—at a nominal fee, of course."

"Of course," Julie said. "You do realize yesterday's excavation was rather gruesome."

"I heard all about it on the news." Millie's smile didn't slip a bit. "People have been calling to get a seat for your talk ever since the story broke. You know, you probably should write up notes before tonight. People will be expecting something interesting."

"Right. Daniel's friend gave me a book yesterday with information on the Meyhew scandal. I suppose I could read through that."

"Marvelous. Let me finish up here with Hannah, and then I can take over the front desk so you can prepare."

Julie settled into the library to try to work, but excited guests popped in frequently, asking her questions and chatting. She barely made it through the story of the Meyhew scandal in the book.

Later that evening, as Julie stepped into the breakfast room, she felt uneasy as she faced the crowd. The whole thing had gotten too big. Too much potential for exposure. She looked over the crowd and nearly stumbled when she recognized several people seated among the group who definitely weren't guests at the inn.

At one table, Steven Needlemeyer sat with his arm around an attractive blond woman. He caught Julie's eye and gave her a friendly nod. She managed a weak smile and nodded back. The woman leaned slightly toward Needlemeyer and whispered. This move drew the attention of the man on the other side of her, Randall Cantor, and his already fierce scowl grew darker.

Julie took another step toward the podium Millie had set at one end of the room and continued her visual sweep of the room. From what she could tell, all of the guests at the inn were present. Her gaze landed on Mrs. Parson, seated at a table with Inga and a man Julie didn't recognize. She could guess his identity easily enough. The man had the carefully styled look of a politician, part distinguished and part slick.

Julie noticed that Inga had changed out of her normal gray attire and into a simple black dress that was more suitable for a funeral. For once, the housekeeper's expression wasn't grim. She gazed at the senator and his wife with a look of near adoration.

Surrounded by sharks. Julie forced a smile and launched into her story of the treasure hunt and the possible murder of Meyhew's wife—a murder he covered up with his tale of her running away with the family fortune. Borrowing some of Shirley's usual storytelling style, she made the story as lurid as possible.

As she spoke, Needlemeyer looked pleasantly interested, as did Cantor's mother. The lawyer's reaction was the polar opposite. His face grew red, and Julie actually saw him clench his fists before he hid them under the table. She half expected the man to make a run at her.

She looked over at the senator's table and was surprised to see him blinking sleepily and taking not-so-subtle glances at his watch. His wife kept her attention fixed politely on Julie, but her face looked melancholy.

When Julie finished, a handful of people hurried to the podium to speak to her, and Julie struggled to keep her suspects in view. The lawyer stood, said something to his mother, and stormed out of the room. He slammed the door to the breakfast room hard enough to make the glass panes rattle.

Julie spoke to each person who crowded around her, answering questions and thanking those who offered compliments. Finally the crowd slipped away, and Mrs. Parson stood and walked to the podium.

"You're a gifted speaker," she said. "But the story is so sad."

"Sad?"

"To think of the poor woman's little son. He couldn't have known what happened to his mama." Mrs. Parson shook her head. "I suppose it's silly to feel for people so long dead." She laughed softly. "Walter says I'm too softhearted."

"I hadn't thought about Mrs. Meyhew's son," Julie admitted. "It must have been horrible for him." Then she smiled at the senator's wife. "And it seems to me that being softhearted is a virtue."

"That's sweet of you to say," Mrs. Parson said, then she

dropped her voice to a whisper. "I should be going. Walter will probably sleep the whole way in the car—not on account of your talk. That was fascinating. Capitol life can just be so exhausting. It's a good thing we have a driver. Good night, dear. Thank you for the wonderful entertainment."

Julie watched the woman walk back to the table and give Inga a hug before leaving with the senator. If the senator was secretly obsessed with the treasure hunt, he certainly did a good job of covering it up, and his wife wasn't exactly the murdering type.

That only left the lawyer. He'd certainly looked ready to kill someone. As Julie gathered up her papers, she decided they needed to kick up their investigation of the angry man, even if it required another bit of breaking and entering.

TWENTY-ONE

Before heading up to bed, Julie decided to talk with Hannah about the lawyer. She found her friend at the kitchen table with a carton of mint chocolate-chip ice cream, a spoon, and a pile of recipe magazines. "All hail the conquering storyteller!"

"I noticed you didn't sit in," Julie said as she grabbed a spoon out of a drawer.

"I've heard the tale, and I was on cleanup duty after the snacks they served before you started. Millie decided we'd sell more goodies *before* you talked about unearthing skulls."

"Did you see Cantor? He had an interesting reaction to my talk. I thought his head would explode."

"He's definitely not a fan of yours."

Julie dug into the ice-cream carton and popped a bite into her mouth, then talked around the mouthful. "We need to know more about him."

Hannah nodded. "Have you read all the stuff I printed out oh so long ago? I had a lot of general stuff on him in that stack, including women he's dated and the various civic functions he's attended. From what I could tell, those were all attempts to troll for new clients."

Julie shuffled her feet. "I haven't quite read all that stuff."

Hannah pinned her with a level stare.

"OK, I haven't quite read *any* of that stuff. I've skimmed a lot of it though. You know I've been busy."

Hannah pointed her spoon at her friend. "You need to learn to do the boring reading bits as well as the exciting illegal-entry bits."

Julie grabbed one more spoonful. "Fine. I'll go read it right now. But in exchange, you need to read through this." She put the old book of Southern scandals on the table next to Hannah. "See what you can get out of it while I go do my homework."

Upstairs, Julie settled down in her cozy chair and pulled the pile of papers into her lap. After the long day, the printed words slowly turned into "blah, blah, blah." Finally she just leafed through, looking for anything interesting in the many printed photos.

She stopped at one of Senator Parson and his wife. They were both younger. The senator had more pepper than salt in his hair then. Mrs. Parson wore the same sweet smile Julie had seen that evening, and the senator looked dashing and proud.

Julie rubbed her eyes and held the paper closer to read the lengthy caption. The text was a little blurry since the photo was a scan taken from the *Straussberg Gazette* and put online. It named one of the local wineries where Parson and his wife were enjoying a wine tasting. It was a puff piece on the popularity of the local vineyards as a honeymoon destination.

Julie grunted softly. The photo simply proved Mrs. Parson had been telling the truth. The Parsons *did* honeymoon in Missouri Wine Country. Julie held the photo close to the light to try to read the rest of the fuzzy print where it gave the newlyweds' names: *Walter Parson and Alicia Meyhew Parson.*

Shocked, Julie dropped the paper on the floor.

She'd finally found the connection! Mrs. Parson was related to the Meyhews. Even so, why would such an old scandal get the Parsons involved now? She thought of the gold coins and jewelry they'd already found. Did Parson need the treasure for his campaign? *Maybe he tried to buy the farm so he could start his own excavation.*

Julie chewed on her lower lip. Something about that felt

like a reach, but she was sure everything that had happened was connected with Mrs. Parson being a Meyhew.

She practically ran downstairs to Hannah's room and pounded on the door. Her friend opened it with the old book in her hand.

"It's Senator Parson!"

"What?"

Julie slipped into Hannah's room and showed her the photo and caption. "Oh wow," Hannah said. "I remember printing that. When I saw how blurry the text was, I didn't bother to read it. You know, that still doesn't prove anything. You don't want to jump ahead too far, or you'll come across like this nut." She held up the book. "Did you read the 'afterword' in this?"

Julie shook her head. "I only read the section on the Meyhew scandal."

"The author's son added an afterword," Hannah explained. "He insists his father was never depressed. The text in this book doesn't sound like a depressed writer's work."

Julie nodded. "He writes like Shirley talks."

"Right, and could you imagine Shirley killing herself in a fit of despondence?" Hannah shook her head. "Anyway, the son said his father planned a whole series of scandal books about different parts of the country. The son says he found his father's body directly after a visit from Meyhew's great-grandson, who was a *doctor*. He hints pretty hard that he thought the good doctor killed his dad."

Julie thought about that and slowly nodded. "Having a murderer for a father-in-law could rock Senator Parson's political boat."

"Especially since we don't know if Jackson Meyhew is alive or dead," Hannah said.

"Louisa said he disappeared."

Hannah flipped a hand dismissively. "It's hard to truly disappear these days. I'll put some time into looking for him if you want."

Julie crossed her arms and leaned on the corner of Hannah's fireplace mantel. "So maybe Alicia Parson comes from generations of murderers. And maybe Parson hired Cantor to keep this all covered up, a job he's clearly not doing well. Having his failure to keep this under wraps displayed right in front of his boss made him angry."

"Perhaps," Hannah said. "It's all speculation."

"But if I'm right and I got the murderer stirred up tonight, Daniel could be in real danger at the dig." Julie pulled out her phone and called him. His phone rolled to voice mail.

"I'm going out there."

"Maybe you should call the police first," Hannah suggested.

"You said yourself that this is all speculation. I have nothing to call them for, but I need to go out there."

"Fine, but as soon as you get there, call me. And put in your earphone so we can talk. If anything happens, I can call 911 and get you some help."

Julie's stomach fluttered during the entire drive to Winkler Farm. She hoped she was being overly imaginative, but too many bad things had happened for her to believe that. She stopped at the bunkhouse and pounded on the door.

No answer.

The inside was completely dark. Julie tapped her foot for a moment, deciding on her next move. She couldn't leave without checking, so she pulled out her lock picks and was inside in moments.

Julie slipped through the small building quickly and found no sign of a struggle. She paused at the door and dialed

Hannah. "I'm inside the bunkhouse. Daniel isn't here."

"He *could* be doing something social, you know."

"I hope so." Julie locked the door behind her and started for her car, but she stopped when she saw a shadow sweep across the ground near her. She turned sharply but didn't see anyone. She watched for the shadow again but saw nothing.

She looked up at the full moon and calculated where someone would have to be to have cast the shadow. Then she headed in that direction. She walked around the bunkhouse and saw a figure racing away, already too distant to make out any details.

"Someone is running toward the dig," Julie said.

"I don't suppose that means you're running the other way."

"Hardly." Julie ran hard, her sneakers pounding the hard ground. She knew both she and the intruder would have to slow down once they reached the mud around the excavation, so she hoped to close the distance between them while she could.

The running figure stumbled when the hard ground softened, and Julie was able to close the distance.

"I know who you are!" Julie yelled.

The person froze and slowly turned to face her.

Despite the jeans and hooded sweatshirt, Julie had no trouble recognizing the face illuminated by the moonlight. She gasped. *How could I have been so wrong?*

"I'll assume by your face that you were bluffing," Mrs. Parson said. Then she removed her hand from the pocket of her sweatshirt and pulled out a small gun. "But then, you're rather adept at telling lies, aren't you, Miss Ellis?"

"I don't know what you mean by that."

"You're not really an innkeeper," Mrs. Parson said, her face twisted in a sneer. "You're a thief."

"As a murderer, I'm not certain that gives you the moral high ground."

"What I did, I did for Walter. You act on your own selfishness."

"And you act like a psychopath from a long line of psychopaths."

The older woman's voice rose to a shriek. "Be quiet! You know nothing about me!"

"I know Meyhew killed his wife."

"My family is not ashamed of our history. My great-great-grandfather killed a harlot to protect his wealth for his son. And his grandson killed a nosy reporter to protect the family name after my father proved too weak for the job." Mrs. Parson shook her head with obvious disappointment at her father's distaste for murder. "He also took care of the son for publishing that filth about the family. How could I not live up to those brave men?"

"But why involve Cantor?"

"I didn't." Mrs. Parson's voice dripped with disgust. "When I told my husband about the problem, he was too spineless to do anything, just like my father. *He* handed the problem off to that incompetent lawyer. Cantor had one job: buy the farm and keep scandal away from our door—and he couldn't even manage *that*."

"Is he the one who vandalized the site?"

The older woman shook her head. "I paid off some of the crew for that, but it didn't help. I had to do something more direct. I decided to destroy the pumps myself. If my family history has taught me anything, it's that sometimes you need to take care of things yourself. The geologist caught me in the act."

"And you killed him."

The woman shrugged. "I did what I needed to do. I always do what I need to do."

"Like attack Daniel."

The other woman simply smiled.

"And now what?" Julie asked. "You shoot me? Don't you think the police are eventually going to track all these dead bodies back to you?"

"To *me*?" she laughed. "Hardly. Everyone loves sweet Mrs. Parson. No, the police will suspect the lawyer after an anonymous tip. Then they'll find poor Randall Cantor dead in his home. The guilt from all these murders will have been too much for him—especially after he kills you and Daniel Franklin."

"Ah. I see. You're copying the family murder cover-ups."

Mrs. Parson's smile twisted. "Going with a classic. I'll take care of that as soon as I finish here. Now, if you don't mind, we'll head back to the bunkhouse. It'll be more convenient if it appears Cantor killed you both together." She waved her gun, stepping closer to Julie.

Julie had been stalling, waiting for the police to arrive. Surely Hannah must have called them. But the look in Mrs. Parson's eyes told Julie that she didn't have much longer to wait. So when Mrs. Parson stumbled slightly on the uneven ground, Julie tackled the older woman, leaping at her and slamming into her waist.

Mrs. Parson went down hard, and the gun flew out of her hand. She clawed at Julie's face with her nails. The older woman was strong. She brought her knees between them and threw Julie off. They both scrambled for the gun in the dark.

"Freeze, Parson! One more inch and I'll shoot!"

Julie collapsed forward in relief as policemen quickly surrounded them. As they hauled Mrs. Parson to her feet, the senator's wife immediately reverted to her sweet society lady persona. "My goodness, I'm so glad you've come! This young woman is insane!"

"Don't bother," Detective Frost said. "I have you on tape."

The older woman's eyes narrowed, but she kept up her gentle façade as they hustled her off to the car.

TWENTY-TWO

The excavation finished as winter set in. More amazing pieces of pre–Civil War history came to light. Daniel was flooded with investors who wanted to contribute to *The Grand Adventure* Steamship Museum in Straussberg.

On the day after the last of the wreck was unearthed, he leaned on the front desk at the inn and offered Julie a wrapped package. "I couldn't have managed this without you."

Julie began to peel the paper from the package. "I'm sure you would have done just fine."

"I'm not even sure I would have survived a week." He leaned close as she opened the box in the wrappings. Inside, a delicate silver dip pen lay nestled in tissue. "It's French. There was a whole shipment of them on the ship. I think the museum can spare just one. You can use it to write your book."

"My book ... yes." Julie smiled. "That's very generous of you."

"I wanted to be sure you didn't forget me, now that all the excitement is over."

"Over? I don't know. It feels like excitement is always right around the corner," Julie said.

Daniel offered a shy smile. "I hope I'll get to share in it with you. I'm looking forward to being in Straussberg as much as possible for a long time."

Julie felt warm clear to her toes. "That's nice to know."

When Daniel left, Millie slipped out of the library. "I didn't want to interrupt anything," she said.

"There was nothing to interrupt."

"That's not how it looked to me."

Julie felt her cheeks flush. "Did you need me?"

"I wanted to tell you that I'll be leaving for Florida in the morning."

"Florida? What happened to Branson?" Julie paused. "Would this change of plans have anything to do with the weather forecasters predicting our first Missouri snow for the year?"

"Maybe a little. I always wanted to run away from the cold Missouri winter. Will you be staying on here?"

Julie looked at her in surprise. "Why wouldn't I?"

Millie snorted. "I'm old, but I'm not senile. You're no innkeeper." Julie started to speak, but Millie held up her hand. "But you do a good job, and the guests are thrilled. I have no desire to get rid of you, but if you get tired of being here, give me a little warning. Don't leave me high and dry."

"I'd never do that."

"Then we're good."

Julie shook her head as Millie trotted up the stairs to pack. She turned back to her work and nearly ran into Inga. The housekeeper had been acting odd ever since Mrs. Parson's arrest. Julie assumed she was mad at her for knocking one of her heroes from her pedestal, but the look on Inga's face wasn't anger.

"Do you have a moment?" Inga asked, her voice a near whisper.

"Of course," Julie said. "You know, I'm sorry about Mrs. Parson. I know you admired her."

Inga shook her head. "I thought I was a good judge of character. I judged Alicia Parson to be a paragon of virtue. And I judged you … harshly."

Julie didn't respond to that. She had no idea what to say.

Inga slowly raised her eyes to meet Julie's. "I must confess

I dug into your past. I thought you were going to bring trouble to the inn, and I love this place. Millie and Shirley are my best friends." She paused, then took a deep breath. "You're not the kind of person I believed you to be when I stitched that message."

"*You* did that?"

Inga nodded, her face a portrait of shame. "I knew your past history was ... checkered. I wanted you to leave before you hurt Millie, so I stitched that message."

"You were being loyal to a friend," Julie said gently. "It was beautiful work, by the way."

"That's not all. When Mrs. Parson asked me to keep an eye on you and report what you did, I did it."

"Oh." No wonder the senator's wife had been eerily well informed about the dig.

"I did what I thought best, given the circumstances," Inga said.

Julie nodded.

The older woman drew herself up to her usual ramrod posture. "I'll keep your secret, about your past. About the trouble you're in. As long as it doesn't threaten Millie." With that, she spun on her heel and walked away.

Julie watched the military precision of the other woman's walk as she disappeared down the hall. After a moment, she shook her head, feeling a smile tug at the corners of her mouth.

She settled down on the stool next to the front desk and took a sip of her lukewarm coffee. Wrinkling her nose at the temperature, she squared her shoulders to face the front entrance. There was no telling what "adventure" might walk through the doors of the Quilt Haus Inn next.

Quilted Vineyard Coasters

Specifications

Finished Coaster Size: Size varies   Number of Coasters: 4
Skill Level: Intermediate

Cutting

Measure wine glass base from side
to side; prepare a circle template 1"
larger than the actual size.

Millie's Vineyard Coasters
Placement Diagram Size Varies

From Print Fat Quarter:

Cut 20 circles for prairie points and
    backings.

From Contrasting Fat Quarter:

Cut 1"-wide bias strips to make 4
    (18") lengths for binding.
Cut 4 circles for linings.

From Thin Batting:

Cut 4 circles.

Assembly

1. Fold 16 print circles into quarter circles to make prairie points
(Figure 1); press.

Figure 1

2. Layer a print circle, wrong side up; a batting circle; a contrasting circle, right side up; and four prairie points with open folds up and corners meeting in the center (Figure 2). Pin to hold.

Figure 2

3. Machine-baste ⅛" from edge all around.

4. Press ¼" to the wrong side on one long edge of a bias strip.

5. Matching raw edges, pin and stitch binding around the edge of the basted coaster on the prairie-point side, overlapping at the beginning and end.

6. Turn the folded edge of the binding to the back side; hand-stitch in place to finish one coaster.

7. Repeat steps 2–6 to complete a total of four coasters.

HELPFUL HINT
• For more detailed help with quilting techniques, go to QuiltersWorld. com and choose Quilting Basics under Quilt Essentials, or consult a complete quilting guide. Your local library may have several on hand that you can review before purchasing one.